ALAMEDA

Steven J Cochron

First published by Coxon Media LLC 2022

First edition

ISBN: 978-1-7376390-6-0

Editing by Aaron Burkholder
Editing by Hannah VanVels Ausbury
Cover art by Rafal Kucharczuk
Design by Liliana Guia

Omar Hernandez looked at the dusty, bottle-cluttered night-stand through one bloodshot eye. The racket he heard banging around in his head was more than a throbbing hangover. Lacking the strength for a proper curse, Omar grunted. With a wild swing, his right hand smacked the area of his nightstand he had zoned as "alarm clock" on the home operating system, trying to turn off the alarm.

To his dismay, the buzzing continued. As Omar became more alert, the menu bar that lived just on the outskirts of his peripheral vision materialized. This time, through sour morning breath, he was able to muster the strength for a solid "FUCK OFF!"

The phone icon in his Heads-Up Display stopped vibrating. Omar rolled over, thinking he would be able to sleep off the rest of the previous night.

The phone started back up again.

Omar checked out the caller ID and recognized the name. *Shit. Work*, he thought.

Security Chief Omar Hernandez struggled to think of the mental command to pick up the phone through his fogged state. Finally, he gave up. Omar gestured with his hands through the air, pantomiming using the phone. As soon as the home operating system recognized what he was doing, it signaled to the nanobots working inside him, and the call connected. The caller, Johnny, was tucked in the upper right corner just next to the phone symbol in Omar's HUD—regardless of whether Omar's eyes were open or not.

He had set his phone up to never stream his own image to the other caller unless he physically turned it on. Which he never did. Johnny was new to the Alameda Security Corp., a subsidiary of CENCOM, and was recently assigned as his lieutenant. Although Johnny thought it odd that Omar did not want to be seen on streams, he had gotten used to it. Most people did not understand why Omar preferred to not stream. All phones were biochipped, anyway. It wasn't like the old days when you dialed a number. Now you dialed the person directly. You couldn't dodge a call by saying "wrong number" even if you wanted to. Sure, you could place the do not disturb option on, but at some point, you had to return the call once you turned that feature off.

Whoever called him regularly would just drop it after a while, learning to expect audio-only... for the most part. He knew that CENCOM Inc., which owned the rights to all streaming inside the former mall, still captured the stream and saved it in the banks, even if they were polite enough not to air it for the caller. By capturing both camera and optical feeds, every inch of Alameda could be digitally captured in a 3-D model in real time. Chief Hernandez had enough of seeing himself streamed from his time with the Force. More than a lifetime's worth, more than a lifetime ago.

As soon as the line connected, Johnny started rambling about a body. Omar started looking for his vape. He couldn't handle a body this early without a hit. Finding the chromatic tube, he checked the cartridge of wolfberry and inhaled. The nanobots, injected at birth, worked very efficiently to keep a person's body operating at peak performance. The bots neutralized all organic methods of getting high. But where there is a need, there is a way. The vape was a gas hack that manipulated the nanobots into getting you off. Omar's wolfberry mix allowed him to not only imbibe alcohol. It also acted as a stimulant. A neat bit of coding that never seemed to last long enough, but it worked. Coursing through him, the wolfberry brought his mind into sharp focus. Chief Hernandez could now hear Johnny clearly.

"Should I call the cops," Johnny asked?

"What was that again, son?"

"We found a body over on Carousel Way. Should I call the cops or wait for you?"

Chief Hernandez flexed his fist a couple of times before bringing it up and rubbing his eye with his knuckle.

"No, don't. Don't wait for me. Call the cops. I'm on my way down now." Omar waved his phone off and reached for last night's glass—a swig of brown liquor to wash out the vape. The moment the warm amber hit his lips, he lurched forward and grabbed his bucket, retching what little he had in his gut.

Omar grabbed his vape along with the pail and headed for the shower. The pounding of his hangover caused his equilibrium to overcorrect. He fumbled to not drop the pail in the shuffle. Kicking yesterday's uniform off into a corner, he hit the vape again. Cool wolfberry rolled over his tongue, settling his stomach, and bringing him back online. Well, as much back to alive as he'd get. The familiar beep signaling the vape was empty chimed. The cartridge was ejected out of the receptacle. Omar pulled it and tossed it on the table with the rest of the empties. How many hits was that? The narcos at Pharma Corp. were getting cheap in their manufacturing.

Omar stepped into his refresher. Again, he fumbled as he figured out which to set down, his pail or vape. He rearranged everything to his left to take a piss with his right hand before closing the toilet in the shower and starting its cleaning cycle. He eyed his pail, considering if he would need it sooner than later, then decided to set it down outside the shower.

Instinctually, he brought his hand to his sides to check the pockets for a fresh cartridge that wasn't there. Omar realized he was naked. He scrambled to find another cartridge sitting on the small table seated in the corner of the room. Omar loaded in a cartridge and hit his vape one more time. He walked back across his room triumphantly and lovingly laid the vape on the shelf next to the shower port.

Omar stretched his body out in the shower to expose as much of his surface area as possible. He placed his hands over the wall markers zoning the shower controls and thumbed the virtual switch. He grinned madly at one of the injecting photo-eyes. A shot of fluoride-infused antiseptic sprayed half his teeth and a good part of his cheek. Licking his lips, he began swishing the cleaner around before spitting it out. He closed his mouth. His naked body was bathed in a mix of light spectrums, chem sprays, and blasts of compressed air. Omar rubbed the chem sprays around to help the more challenging to reach armpits and crack. The whole process took only seconds.

Once, when Chief Hernandez was still a member of the Tactical Peace Brigade, he had won a night at a local pleasure palace and took a hot shower there. Since water was only used for kitchen work, most people had never experienced such luxury. He didn't think they were missing much. The hot, steaming streams of water stung his skin and didn't feel very clean to him. You got out still wet and had to use a cloth to finish the job. The working girl Omar was with that night said many of her more affluent clients rented the room just for the shower alone. It wasn't for him.

Chief Hernandez looked in the mirror and decided he could go without a shave one more day. Tomorrow would be another story. Stepping out of the shower, he accidentally kicked the pail. Cursing a short prayer of thanks, it didn't spill over as the pail slid across the tiled floor of the refresher. Omar picked it up and carried it over to the sink with wall features for cleaning. He dumped the bucket down the small drain and worked the virtual controls on the tiled space for a cleaner. His pail got a short blast of solution. The new bile mix swished around before he dumped it down the drain. One more shot, and it was ready for the next hard morning after a long night.

Chief Hernandez got dressed. Putting his shirt on triggered the automated response that reminded him there were ten days left until the subscription for the uniform needed to be renewed. He clicked the okay icon and went about the task of pulling his pants up. The reminders were annoying as the subscription was paid routinely through Omar's credited account managed by Alameda Security Accounts Payable Department's AI.

When new, the uniform had been a dark gray. Now it was almost white from all the cleanings. He attached his belt, which hung loose, and he had to go down another notch. He sized himself up in the mirror. The shirt, even tucked, hung limply. He sat on the edge of the bed as he slid on his old boots and zipped them up. Long gone were days of buff and shined parade standard. The worn leather felt paper-thin, and the soles were more glue and used tire tread than an original heel.

Chief Hernandez picked up his personal AC and hung it around his neck. Years back, Alameda's air conditioning broke. The filters still worked, and it cycled air through but didn't cool any of it down. Instead of fixing the AC, CENCOM rented out individual AC units to the residents. Online state-of-the-art air conditioning. It worked wonders on a hot day. All of it billed along with rent. Everyone living in Alameda had at one point commented how they wished they had just shut off the hot air blowing from one end to the other. Unfortunately, it was the only way for the filters to keep the air clean enough to breathe.

Omar eyed his gun lying on his table across the small single room. It was still holstered. A promising sign he hadn't been too stupid the night before.

Carrying a gun was optional while working. Some days he did. Some days he didn't. To Omar, he really didn't have any particular preference. With how hungover he felt, he decided not to buckle on the holster.

He tapped a small square to the side of the door, signaling for the lights. Grabbing his RFID keys, he exited his room. He had been living there for thirteen years. It was a simple ten by ten room with a shower drop-down toilet/sink combo in one corner. It was very basic but a step up from a pod. Chief Hernandez resided on the second floor in the middle of the mall's south wing. It was no more than a bed, a couple of small chairs, and no windows. He ate at several cafés for free as partial payment for his position. That negated the need for a kitchen. He didn't know how to cook anyway, so it never bothered him.

Outside of his quarters, Omar looked up and down the corridor wall. The five by four by three-foot pods stacked two high choked every free space that was not zoned for a byway. The pods were just big enough to hold one person. That is, if they didn't stretch out. The old play on words was "five, four, three, too one," and someone would groan and give you the bird. Over the years, it was just shortened to "one" or "one-er." Outsiders may try to pull off a weiner slur, but that usually ends with the outsider getting a skull correction or an earful of profanity-laced Spanglish if from a woman. *Well, most women*, Omar thought with a chuckle. Most outsiders weren't as tough as a mall resident, and Omar wouldn't be surprised to see one of the female persuasion knock the shit out of an outsider—woman or man. It was a truth wherever you went. People were more formidable at the bottom of the heap than at the top.

The most common slur for people who lived here was mall rat, and boy, you'd better hope a local never heard you utter that shit. You'd get more than a "correction." First, the place hadn't been a mall for decades. Second, people never like to be called rats.

As Omar walked down the byway, folks were just waking up for the day. Omar felt fortunate that he had his own shower and didn't have to queue up for one in the morning. Sun spilled through long stretches of skylights that dotted the ceiling along the walkway. The long stretch of walls was at one time beige, which you could see small traces of between the cracks between pods. In between the rows of pods was a door every eleven feet or so. The door housed other members of Alameda that could afford to live there. The worn and tarnished red brick floor clapped against his heels as Omar walked.

At the end of the corridor was a small CENCOM caffeine station run by Mrs. Walker. She made a decent cup of coffee—if you could afford it. It was almost the whole bean. His free meals didn't include luxury items like coffee, so Omar only got it when he needed it. He never asked Mrs. Walker where she got the coffee beans. All coffee shops this low in the social hierarchy had to infuse chicory root into whatever used beans they could get their hands on. Most people resorted to synthetic caffeine options.

The Incan Confederacy was strangling the coffee supply throughout the world. The IC claimed that it was due to global warming. Forced scarcity for profit is what the news streamers called it. That left most pick-me-ups of the chemical variety. Omar had decided that most chemical cocktails for caffeine just didn't compare to coffee for hangovers. At the beginning of every month, Omar purchased augmented coffee tokens from Mrs. Walker. When he ran out, he ran out. The tokens were of Mrs. Walker's own design—simple, as she was a small-time coffee stand renter, but effective. On one side of the bronze-colored coins was a paper cup filled with an infinite coffee stream. The other side had the volume of its worth. The tokens Omar bought were only worth one hundred and twenty milliliters.

"Morning, Mrs. Walker. Coffee, please." Omar pulled the token from his HUD's inventory and dropped it on Mrs.

Walker's counter. The coin stood upright, spinning, waiting for Mrs. Walker to pick it up.

"You wouldn't have a little something to warm it up, would you?"

Mrs. Walker eyed him. She had figured out long ago why Omar got coffee on certain days. "Sure thing, Omar. Five credits."

Omar grinned slightly as a faint jingle rang in his ear, notifying him that his account was charged for the infusion. "Confirmed correct. Thanks." A new balance appeared and then disappeared in a flash from his HUD.

Mrs. Walker pulled out a bottle of clear liquid and set it on the counter as the coffee was poured. *Looks like vodka today*, Omar thought.

"You ever worry CENCOM will shut you down for that? I mean, you're being a little brazen leaving the bottle on the counter like that."

"I'm not doing anything wrong, Chief. What do I need to hide?"

He turned around and walked over to the railing. Looking down at the main floor, he took an inventory of what he saw. People were climbing out of their pods. They would either head over to queue up for a shower or simply head off to work—the slow transition from the stillness of the night to the bustle of a full house.

"Cup's ready, Omar."

"Thanks," he muttered as he picked up his order and walked to the stairs.

While sipping the cup of joe, he nodded good morning to the passersby heading off to jobs outside the complex. The byway's overhead lights were still dim, but the bright amber morning sun didn't seem to care about Omar's hangover. The heavier-than-usual northbound traffic below let him know that Johnny must have closed off the south exit. The southbound exit was one of the most popular exits. *People are going to be late to work today*, Chief Hernandez thought.

Chief Hernandez threaded his way through people, passing between pods that lined every inch of the fairway. The automation of all farm labor plus the complete collapse of major cities had created a migration of human suffering to the Central Valley not seen since the Great Depression more than two hundred years earlier. If it wasn't for the massive desalination plants off the coast, there would have been no way anyone could live in the Central Valley—or anywhere in California, for that matter. They all would have died of thirst long ago. The mall gave shelter from the harsh, blistering days in the San Joaquin.

Carousel Way was at the southern tip of Alameda. A large group had started forming around the scene. Omar felt unease as he passed through the crowd. Something was amiss. Bodies found in the mall were a weekly occurrence. It was always an outsider who'd OD'd on a poorly coded hit. Chief Hernandez liked that the mall was self-regulating regarding outsiders and drugs. His position was mainly ceremonial for CENCOM, the mall's owner.

CENCOM used to be known as Central Communication Inc., which revolutionized communication by linking all people via a network of nanobots. CENCOM owned all of the housing in the Central Valley. If you couldn't afford to rent one of CENCOM's houses, they would rent you a pod. All former malls, now defunct, had been converted to communal living facilities. Along with office buildings no longer needed for office work, auto shops, and any other brick-and-mortar building that was no longer needed for its original intention was transformed into a new purpose. It was part of CENCOM's humanitarian outreach projects, their attempt at cleaning up the streets.

CENCOM may not have known that the residents actually enforced the law in Alameda. Each facility was made up of several communities. At the head of these communities sat a Sponsor. The Sponsors formed what was called a Tribunal. The Tribunal was the governing body of the residence community. Tribunal Sponsors kept the riffraff out of their smaller, sub-communities. The Tribunal agreed that peace was best for everyone. At least in Alameda. There was no infighting for resources. The Tribunal's engagement to their respected site depended on who sat on each panel. Even with all this cooperation, some facilities relied more on CENCOM security than others.

If a junky outsider came in looking for trouble, Chief Hernandez or one of the other security officers would be asked to handle it quietly. That isn't to say that it wasn't okay to get off in the mall, just not if you were going to be an asshole about it. Especially if you were from the outside. If a disturbance came from a resident? Well, they were exiled until they got their shit together per the Tribunal's practice. The exiled would be handled before Chief Hernandez had to step in. Unless he was requested to escort someone out. It was practically unheard of for any local to be found iced in the mall, barring domestic disputes. Outside the mall was another story. News reports streamed that the podless killed each other daily. Fear of banishment kept people in line.

Chief Hernandez's day-to-day mainly consisted of petty theft among those that lived on the main fairway or byway. The fairway that ran down the center of Alameda and the overhead byway was not considered a part of any one of the smaller sub-communities. A majority of the fairway residents were eager to join a sub-community, so they kept to themselves and kept their noses clean, hoping that a spot would open up.

Chief Hernandez got to the front of the pack and saw Johnny placating and holding back the crowd. Johnny was in his late twenties. A heavy-set man whose frame was built for security, he held himself with a confident demeanor that projected authority. Yet, the face resting in his oval-shaped head held compassionate eyes that worked for Johnny when he had to defuse a hostile situation. As Johnny spoke, the crowd listened.

Seeing Omar approach, Johnny flagged one of the other security officers to take his place and escorted the chief up to the body. At first glance, it didn't seem like much. A dingy blue and silver tarp loosely covered something lying flat against the waxed and polished red brick wall and floor. It could've been anyone wandering in, trying to avoid paying rent for a night. At night, every so often, a podless would hop over the security fence surrounding the compound and snake their way in and squat until a patrol spotted them and ushered them along. The area around the doors—large opaque windows—was kept clear by residents who didn't want a pod exposed to the sun during the day. The closer to the door the pod was, the lower the rent. A twenty-foot-deep area right next to the doors was void of pods altogether.

Omar could do the mental math. If he was called at around six in the morning, somewhere between 5:05 and 5:55 the body had shown up. They both squatted down as Omar started to take a closer look. Then he saw the hand. Small, elegant, clean nails. Omar sniffed and noticed the lack of smell.

"She's not a junkie, is she?"

"Afraid not, Chief," Johnny answered.

"You guys cover her up?"

"No. Found her as is."

"Fuck," Omar grumbled.

He instinctually gloved and masked up to take a closer look. Then, gently pulling back the tarp, Chief Hernandez saw the victim's face.

"Is that Lucia?" someone from the crowd yelled out.

Johnny jumped up to help get the crowd back as Chief Hernandez looked her over. It was Lucia. She looked like someone had tried to wash her down. The smeared makeup with wet hair complemented the sea of red that used to be the eyes. Her face was bespectacled with burst capillaries, and there was bruising around her neck. A split lip and a series of bruises along the right side of her face told him someone left-handed had worked her over first.

Omar gently covered her face back up and stood looking down at the young woman. Lucia wasn't a pro, nor was she a junkie. She was a terrific young lady, one who everyone knew.

People tended to gravitate towards the strong and intelligent, and Lucia was both. Growing up in the mall, she was an exceptional student. Many of the kids had her as a tutor at one time or another. She was a rising star that was supposed to get out of the mall and become something. She had graduated with a master's in science from a prestigious online school. She was supposed to be working towards some kind of doctorate. All that and Lucia wasn't even thirty yet. Omar had done as well as was expected of himself in school before joining the military. Many of the mall's population was on par with him—just enough schooling to be accepted into a trade.

There was a bit of hero worship for individuals like Lucia, who could climb the higher rungs of education. But even with all that going for her, she had decided to stay in the mall and continue to help her community. Working long hours in the communal vertical gardens helped feed mall residents. She advised many in times of need. If she did not eventually replace a Sponsor, the residents of the mall would have created a new spot for her on the Tribunal.

The soft melody in Omar's ear had him looking reflexively at the caller ID in the corner of his HUD. The call was coming in from Tac's investigative squad. Tac was the local private security firm that policed the area. During the Uber Depression, social unrest grew towards public police forces that had appeared out of control. Cities had to downsize local police and their overpriced unions, switching instead to private security firms. Sixty-some-odd years of foreign and domestic wars in what used to be called the US had created many unemployed fighters who were trainable. Omar used to be one himself. Fresno's firm was initially called Tactical Peace Force. TPF was made up of new recruits from the collapsed US armed forces and local police officers who decided to stay in town. When CENCOM acquired the Force, it rebranded TPF to Tactical Peace Brigade—to soften its image—which was later boiled down to just Tac. Apparently, people thought TPB was a mouthful.

By now, Omar should have received a form email with several different feeds attached to it showing the murder and body dump from different viewpoints for his report. Including a disturbing feed of the last thing Lucia saw before she died when her implants stopped feeding to her cloud storage.

"Chief Hernandez here," he answered.

A middle-aged woman was sitting behind a desk. Staring blankly at the air, she began a familiar song and dance to Omar.

"Are you sure? Your image isn't showing. I'll hang up and try again."

"No, it's fine. I block my stream from popping up. Can I help you?"

"Oh." A perplexed look washed over her face for a moment before she steeled herself and continued. "Security Chief Hernandez? My name is Detective De La Torre. My office received a call from one of your security patrolmen regarding a body. Are you at the location now?"

Looking at the ornate brick wall in front of him, Omar scratched at the back of his neck. "Yes, ma'am. I was just about—"

"Detective."

"Excuse me, ma'am?"

"No, ma'am. Just Detective, please."

"Right. Detective. As I was saying, I was just about to send for the bus before heading over to fill out the forms. Do you happen to have the stream for my report yet?'"

"That's why I'm calling, Chief Hernandez. We don't have any feed coming out of the area from 5:15 to 5:45. Thirty minutes of dead air with no report as to why. I wanted to inform you that my partner and I are coming down. Have the area cordoned off, and don't touch anything. We'll be down there as soon as I finish filing the paperwork for authorization."

"Hmm-mm." Omar took a hit of wolfberry and let out a long exhale. "Look, Detective, it's going to be a hot one today. Lucia is right by the window. Everyone down here would be pretty upset if I left her out."

"Not a hair, Chief. We're on our way."

She switched off, leaving Omar staring at the wall. After another hit of wolfberry, he turned to Johnny.

"Call the coroner down here, but don't let them touch or move the body. If the detectives aren't down here by say… 11, do a bio-scan and let the coroner take her."

"Yes, Chief. Why's it taking so long?"

"Paperwork. Speaking of which, I need to go start mine. There was a loss on the feed that I'll have to report, too. Then I'll need to report the loss to Lucia's Sponsor." Chief Hernandez was about to walk away. His HUD rang. Chief Hernandez checked the corner to see that his boss was calling.

"Good morning, Commander. How can I help you?"

"Morning, Chief. A report came in that you have a dead body this morning?"

"News travels fast. Yes, I was on my way to start the reports."

"Great. Hey, look. End-of-quarter budgets reports are coming in. Can you wrap this up quickly? Alameda's expenses seemed high, and we're at risk of coming in over budget."

Omar hesitated before answering. He was aware that, in all likelihood, someone in the audience could hear his response. Even if they only heard one side of the conversation.

"We always do our best, Commander, but… ah… this death may take a little more. She's not a normal type of victim."

"Chief, what's normal when it comes to death? Just send in the reports and hand everything over to the detectives as fast as possible."

"Yes, sir."

The feed was dropped, and Omar doublechecked to make sure the line was clear.

As Omar turned from the brick wall he was staring at, he mumbled. "Fucking prick."

"You say something to me, Chief?" asked Johnny.

"No, nothing. I'm going to take care of the reports. Hey, you hear anything?" The chief gestured to the young woman's body.

"No, Chief. Things have been quiet. And besides, she never got into any trouble that I know of. She was well-liked."

"Yeah, that's what I thought. Okay, thanks."

7:23 a.m.

Omar made his way to the re-pub he was authorized to work from. A few of the old mall's shops had been converted to remote public offices or re-pub as they were sometimes called. CENCOM owned them all but you could rent a seat. All office work that was not automated was done remotely except for the super affluent who flaunted their face-to-face office space. Everyone knew that office spaces were a waste of corporate funds. However, private owners who could afford it would pay top dollar for an office space to show how successful they had become. Ironically, any company with a CEO instead of a corporate AI running things never saw that CEO in person. Why commute when augmented reality streams were so much faster, and cheaper? The re-pubs had started during the dark decade of the Uber Depression. Sparked from the first coronavirus that swept the globe back in the '20s. First, shelter-in-place drove a lot of workers from the offices. Then several years later, the collapse of the global economy. Nobody could afford the office space. Everyone had to tighten their belt. Omar had learned in school that many people didn't want to leave their homes regardless of the cure due to rioting and social unrest. Regardless of the reasons, mega-corps had a new way to save money, and start-ups couldn't afford the space.

So, the re-pub was created out of necessity for consistent net access that was cost-effective. Rooms of people sitting in row after row facing straight ahead. Eyelids relaxed or fluttering, hands resting comfortably on their laps. The neuro-link user integration worked from thought instead of the outdated physical act of pantomime. Packed in as tightly as the proprietor was legally allowed. Lights kept dim to not interfere with what they were trying to read, type, or input. Worn carpet, bare walls, a caffeine station, and a bathroom were pretty much what was expected in most re-pubs. Alameda's re-pubs only offered a bathroom. A caffeine station would be too costly for most employees working in mall re-pubs. CENCOM tended to tear them out to add more chairs and the smaller water bottle-filling station. The cost of the re-pub was tax-deductible to the drones, unless one worked for a rare company that allowed employees to expense their rental of the space. Most companies assumed your workspace was your business. You either performed the job or the corporations found someone else to do it. With three-fourths of the population unemployed, drones were cheaper than AIs.

With the AC dead, the re-pub was steamy. Even this early in the morning. These mall sections were scorching hot during the summer and freezing during the winter, as climate control was an unnecessary expense. There was a kiosk that rented out the personal climate units you hung around your neck made by one of CENCOM's subsidiaries. Of course, the kiosk was also owned by CENCOM. Throughout the mall, every storefront was owned or controlled by CENCOM. Even the social workers' offices the state required to be present in the living facility were subcontracted through CENCOM.

Omar had sweat through the fresh uniform during the short walk from the crime scene to the re-pub. His body was trying to push out everything he had poured into it the previous night. He undid the top two buttons of his shirt while climbing a small ramp to the atrium and finished his coffee before depositing the cup in a bin.

Walking through Alameda was like walking through a mix of barracks and bazaars. Used and repurposed goods available to rent were laid out on carpets or tables for passersby to look through. These makeshift kiosks were crammed between any space they could fit. Some ran right out of their pod. A river of humanity was constantly coming and going. Residents simply hung out of their pods, legs dangling as they watched the comings and goings. Some with their pods flap down, sitting and staring off into the distance while focusing on whatever stream crossed their eyes.

The smell of body odor was relentless. It permeated everything. Incense sticks burned every couple of meters. The mix of different scents created a new sickly-sweet aroma that never actually drove the BO away. Soot and ash from the sticks covered everything.

As Omar walked through the crowd, those doing business not entirely on the up and up would spot Omar and try to tuck away what contraband they had. Usually, some form of moonshine or low-grade coded vape. It amused Omar when they tried to hide the vape when there was a giant cloud blowing above their heads. The illicit market brought a good deal of outsiders to the fairway. That traffic helped drive sales of more legitimate businesses. Because of that, Chief Hernandez and his officers tended to look the other way.

Omar glanced up at the sign outside a re-pub and took a hit from his vape. A hand-drawn sign that read "Bananas Re-Pub, a personal space while you work in your virtual place" hung over the tinted windows that made up the front. Omar squinted past the darkness.

The room wasn't packed as of yet. However, even this early, some people were already online. Fritz, the manager and one of the few residents Omar considered a friend, sat in one of the chairs in the back. Fritz's job would only require him for new clients, allowing him to spend most of his time working on his real calling as an amateur e-sports star. An AI could have easily replaced him, but federal law mandated an onsite warm body.

Fritz was a scrawny, brown-haired, blue-eyed forty-something who just couldn't figure it out. In high school, he had been captain of his e-sports team. He had been good enough to take his team all the way to state. However, not much else happened for Fritz. Fritz never earned a scholarship, even with the state championship under his belt. His grades weren't good enough to continue any other education, and he was forced into playing the amateur circuit. For a hot minute, he tried his hand at being a commentator, but he had no personality. No one wanted to tune in to see a two-dimensional has-been who never was commenting on actual stars. As time went on and Fritz's reflexes waned, he fell further and further into obscurity. Whenever Fritz wasn't online, he could be found down at the bar getting drunk, reliving his glory days to anyone who would listen.

Fritz wasn't that bad of a guy. He was washed up, but he was fun to hang out with. Fritz kept to himself for the most part. Never getting into any more trouble than the occasional one too many drinks at the bar requiring him to need an escort to his pod.

Omar sent a text.

[Chief.Sec.O.HERNANDEZ]: Morning @FreakyFritzFree-loader. I need the chair.

No reply.

Chief Hernandez was careful not to disturb the other tenants as he made his way through the stations towards the back. Some were residents of the mall he recognized. Some were outsiders. Halfway through the room, he sent another text.

[Chief.Sec.O.HERNANDEZ]: Hey! @FreakyFritzFree-loader. I need the chair.

Omar waited patiently for Fritz to log out.

[FreakyFritzFreeloader]: Not now, Chief. I'm busy. Give me 30?

[Chief.Sec.O.HERNANDEZ]: Can't. It's urgent.

[FreakyFritzFreeloader]: Just a little bit longer! We've almost got the objective.

[Chief.Sec.O.HERNANDEZ]: Freak. I will pull your god-damn license if you don't get out of my chair. NOW!

Fritz opened his eyes and stood up.

"Jesus, Omar. What's the rush?" Fritz whispered.

"Someone iced Lucia last night."

Quickening his step, Fritz got out of the way so Omar could log in. "No shit?"

"No shit."

Omar was in before his back had fully leaned into the chair, going through security protocols authorizing his status for the CENCOM servers. The re-pub's connection boost made it faster for him to navigate the complex series of thoughts that selected various apps and files.

He requested diagnostics on the feeds by Carousel Way and figured he might also do the ones in the parking lot. While he waited for the system to report results, he inquired about the time frame Detective De La Torre had mentioned, seeing for himself. Sure enough, any feed in the entrance area was cut out right at 5:15 and didn't return until 5:45. Looking at the parking lot footage, he noticed something interesting. The feed in the parking lot dropped before the entrance feed by a good twenty minutes, returned for thirty minutes, then dropped again at 5:45 for another five minutes. He watched and re-watched the thirty-minute feeds from the parking lot at three times the speed. He wasn't sure, but he thought he could make out someone putting the body down from one of the cameras pointing at the doors across the lot. Omar saved what little footage he had to a new file on his personal server. He would hand it over to the detectives and maybe even have someone he knew check it out. The diagnostics were still running, so he started filling out the form for a dead body on the premises, then the form for picking up a body, and finally, the forms for losing a resident.

Before he finished the final form, he was notified that the results were in and brought up the attached file.

CENCOM INC.

DIAGNOSTICS REPORT
MALL HOUSING FACILITY
LOCATION: CA 93726
FACILITY #3-03452978224
ZONE: SOUTH ENTRANCE CAROUSEL WAY
ZONE: SOUTH PARKING STRUCTURE

REPORT: All feed functioning according to design. Tested feed brought back positive results of functionality. No anomalies were detected. Reported time of issues analyzed. Feed recorded. Footage classification code [sec7-58426-265a]. Storage location classified. Scheduled for deletion. Mandatory 24-hour hold.

END REPORT

Chief Hernandez quickly noted the codes and saved the report to the file he created. Looking at the time, he realized he'd been on for over two hours, which gave him and the detectives under nineteen hours to get their hands on the missing feed. Omar sent in a request to halt the deletion and a request for code clarification. He shared the file with the detectives and texted Lucia's Sponsor.

[Chief.Sec.O.HERNANDEZ]: @TheGrandDutchessOfDesh
On my way to speak with you.

Omar logged out and got out of the chair. Fritz, eyes fluttering, was squatted with his back against the wall. The room was full of drones murmuring as they worked. Busy bees buzzing about their work. Omar kicked Fritz's legs out from under him as he made his way out the door.

Fritz hushed a yell. "What was that for?"

"For making me wait," Omar shot back over his shoulder while flipping Fritz the bird and cracking a smile.

Fritz playfully shot back a cupped hand pumping across his own crotch, flicking his thumb out at the end of the motion.

Emerging from the darkened re-pub, Chief Hernandez could feel the immediate wash of emotion that hung in the air. The hustle and bustle of the mall felt weighted with a sadness that seemed to cling to the walls like morning dew. An audible shift in tone hit him, dampening the typical range of sounds from people in the byway that usually continually reverberated, filling the air all the way to the second story ceiling above. Eyes watched him a few beats too long before returning to their everyday conversations as he walked by. His sense of time paused, then sped back up. He gulped, then took a hit of wolfberry. *Beep.* The cartridge ejected, and mindlessly he swapped it out with one from his pocket.

Maybe he just imagined the shift and the eyes lingering on him. A prickle ran up his spine. Omar continued to make his way to the north quarters where Lucia had her pod. Her Sponsor, Lady Desh, would be waiting for him to report.

Everywhere he looked as he walked, signs were going up in remembrance of Lucia. The word had clearly gotten out. Mourning ribbons of black were being passed around along with armbands and white plastic carnations. It was a rare sight. Although death was a persistent note in the chorus that was mall life, a sense of actual loss of Lucia was felt by all. Chief Hernandez had no dealings with the young woman himself. He just knew of her. Knew of her work in the community. A beacon of light others tended to draw towards. Omar didn't run in such circles. His was for the mad and damned.

A warning sign to most. A gatekeeper for the outliers on their way to hell. Used up and ready for bed. He didn't know how to handle Lucia or the sense of loss he felt for someone he didn't know. He continued down the fairway towards Lucia's pod that was housed in El Corazon Block.

Lucia's Sponsor, Lady Desh, was one of the three Sponsors of the Alameda Tribunal. She was a ferociously compassionate outspoken leader of the housing block known as El Corazon.

Lady Desh was a sight to see. She possessed a beauty that could still be perceived through the dark veil she wore at all times to hide the scars from her youth. Once a predominant influencer, with hundreds of millions of followers worldwide, she went by the handle the Grand Duchess of Desh.

Ten years ago, Lady Desh was attacked by a female stalker when she did not reciprocate the super fan's advances. The stalker splashed acid across the Grand Duchess of Desh's face. The stalker was caught by other fans before the police could get to her and was promptly torn apart, limb by limb. Literally. There are darknet sites where you can download and replay the brutal mob killing through the eyes of several of the participants. For a fee, of course.

The Grand Duchess of Desh was immediately rushed to the hospital. Weeks of international mourning culminated with the announcement of the Grand Duchess of Desh's retirement from public life. Too hideously injured to go on, she eventually found refuge in Alameda, becoming a vital, outspoken resident who rose to become a member of the Tribunal. She became known simply as Lady Desh to everyone in Alameda. Afterward, she committed to sweeping reforms that encouraged order for the families in the community. How someone so wealthy stayed in the mall was beyond Omar's comprehension. Nevertheless, she never left, focusing all her time and attention on the residents. She never flaunted her wealth over anyone, having an air of languid grace and demonstrated the epitome of compassion.

El Corazon Block operated with traditional monogamist norms for marriage. The community's bylaws allowed for families to create polyamorous marriage contracts, but monogamy was the predominant model. Marriage, of course, allowed for families, regardless of dynamic, to receive benefits within the pods. Combining pods to create a larger living space and increased power access were just two of the perks. An individual or family didn't have to join a sub-community. However, sub-communities like El Corazon granted access to increased safety, more resources, and the ultimate perk—privacy.

A little over ten thousand people lived in the mall, with the lion's share living in the sub-communities. Renovated from the old Gottschalks retail store, El Corazon was the most prominent structure attached to the main fairway of the mall. It resided in the mall's center, lending it its name as the heart. The main entrance was on the ground floor, but another entrance was on the second floor along the byway. There were, of course, exits and loading doors that led to the exterior on the other side of the building, used exclusively by El Corazon's residents. Any external exits would've been heavily guarded against outside vagrants if not permanently sealed. There were only three entrances into the mall for oneers and outsiders—the south end entrance and the two on the west end. The historic north entrance to the mall ran through the Machinist Guild's territory. And was sealed shut by them. Omar squeezed by the rows of pods and fairway occupancy on his way to El Corazon. The fairway was filling with people and harder to navigate.

An old peddler came up and handed Omar a flier with a black armband.

"*Para su jefe, Hernández. En memoria de Lucía.*"

"*Gracias, señor.*" He quickly put the band on his left arm as the man nodded and continued passing out armbands. A memorial service had already been scheduled for this evening. Although not a surprise, it was impressive to Omar how quickly the community reacted.

He heard a tune in the air. It was familiar, but he could not quite put his finger on it. A lone flute behind the everyday hustle and bustle of the byway. The red brick tiles that lined the floors and walls carried the soft tune in the air. Omar looked around but couldn't find the player. He had reached El Corazon.

Omar waved to the enforcer seated at his station at the entrance of El Corazon. The enforcer was one of his off-duty guards. All three sub-communities in Alameda had some form of extra security at the entrances of that group's central living cluster. The enforcer's eyes were red from tears.

The layout of El Corazon's entrance was such that when entering the quarters, you were immediately greeted by a wall of stacked pods. This wall forced you to turn right or left down a narrow three-foot-wide corridor. Two pods' lengths later, the path had you turning inward into the rest of the community. Like the byway, the inner circle had walls lined with pods. Unlike the byway, pods not attached to the wall were organized by pushing two or three pods together and stacked higher. Some pods were stacked four high—like trans-galactic containers on ships returning from Alpha Centauri to the docks of Luna City. And just as colorful, too. Pods were made from cheap, mass-produced aluminum shells. Not to protect the occupant from the elements but to help lock and secure the contents from would-be thieves. The cheap quality of the pods allowed for the opportunity for the residents to modify them if desired. It wasn't legal according to the leases on the pods. Still, modifications were never penalized as long as the pods were leasable and CENCOM didn't lose any revenue.

And so, clusters of pods were modified uniquely to their

family's needs. Interior walls removed, structures reinforced, a small window added lighting. Crawl spaces hung overhead like a giant hamster cage. They all had some personalization not seen in the byway. Walls painted or wallpapered. Curtains and drapes instead of roll-up doors. Netting for storage hung from ceilings.

The groupings formed four blocks with the same narrow walkway between each one. In the center was a walkway twice the width of the other passages, crisscrossing with other narrow alleyways, all leading to the open center of El Corazon. It felt both suffocating and like being safely back in the womb all at the same time. Soft, muffled crying could be heard. A weighted sense of pain washed over Omar. Each step forward felt heavier than the last. The heart of El Corazon was a small open square adorned with several collapsible tables and chairs. On either side of the small square were stairs leading to the second floor that housed even more community members. The last of the morning's residents were in the process of finishing up their breakfast. At the far end of the circle, Omar spotted Lady Desh and her wife, Cynthia, tending to a group of small children.

Lady Desh glided through the children. Not having children of their own, the lady and her spouse doted over the children in the community like they were their own. Noticing Omar enter the communal dining area, Lady Desh gestured for him to sit in a corner where they would get some privacy.

"Have a seat there, please, Chief Hernandez." She turned to a stack next to her and picked up a plate. "Have you eaten yet, Chief?"

"No." Omar sat quietly with his hands on his lap. Cynthia came by and set down some silverware, a cup, and a pitcher of chilled water. She nodded at Omar. Omar looked around uncomfortably. What few people there were in the area were quiet and barely picking at what was on their plates.

"Not a lot of appetites this morning, Chief." Lady Desh came over and set down a plate—a substantial portion of upma topped with diced and chopped veggies, a couple of pieces of naan, and a small spoonful of chorizo and eggs. "You can eat before we begin if you like."

"Thank you. That is very kind of you. Perhaps you could tell me more about Lucia while I eat?"

"Certainly."

Omar began tearing off naan and using it as a spoon to shovel a mixture of upma and eggs. He hadn't realized how hungry he had gotten. Omar washed down the first spicy mouthful with cool water before eagerly spooning in more. This close through the veil, Omar could see a pleased look appear on Lady Desh. Fifteen years his junior, she looked at him as a caring mother looking upon a small child. She allowed him to slow down before continuing.

"Lucia and her father joined Alameda about nine or ten years ago. Lucia's father was able to get the family into El Corazon fairly quickly if I remember correctly. Her mother had died of cancer, I think. Her father was murdered coming home from work during the strikes several years back. She began working in our gardens to keep up on her dues for her pod. She wisely downsized whenever she could. She was very frugal. She took to the gardens naturally, which is why she is…" Lady Desh trailed for a moment. Her hand came up under her veil, wiping a tear. "Sorry. *Was*. She *was* studying agriculture at the university. She didn't sit around much like many of her age playing online. She kept herself busy in real-ity. If she wasn't at school or in one of the gardens, you could find her helping one of the kids. She had an old soul, as they used to say. Many, young and old, came to her for advice. She often was the first to volunteer for holiday programs for the community. She was a pillar."

"Was she seeing anyone?"

"A boy here and there occasionally but not currently, I don't think. Not really anyone's business. You know?"

"Hmm. Anyone close she may have confided in?"

"As much as she was there for others. I'm afraid she never got too close to anyone."

Chief Hernandez finished his food and cleared his throat with another long pull of water. "Lady Desh, was anyone mad at her? Did she have any enemies?"

"Omar, what's going on?" she asked nervously. Omar began to pick at a faded sticker on the plastic gray folding table.

"We don't have any footage of what happened."

Lady Desh was shocked. "So you don't know what happened?"

"Afraid not. There's some kind of weird security code attached to it. I'm looking in to find out why."

There was a long pause as Lady Desh collected herself.

"No one here, Chief. I can't speak for the university, though."

"On-campus work? Why not online like everyone else?"

"She was working on a doctorate and needed access to the university labs. She continued to live here instead of on the campus. Maybe you should come with me, Chief. And see what she was working on in the garden."

"Okay, but I'd like to look at her pod first."

"Of course."

Chief Hernandez and Lady Desh rose from their seats. Lady Desh turned to a small group of kids. In a mix of Spanish and Punjabi, the Lady Desh called out.

"Sara, *limpia 'tē pakavāna de la mesa*." A young girl came over and cleared the dishes from the table.

"*Gracias, señorita*," Chief Hernandez thanked the girl.

Lady Desh led the chief towards the stairs on the far south edge of the atrium.

"As I was commenting, Lucia was frugal. She moved up to the second floor, where pods are cheaper due to residents not wanting to climb stairs regularly, as well as a lack of automation."

"A lack of automation?"

"When they automated the housing operating system to full augmentation, they skipped on the number of cameras needed to fully implement the second floor. Cutting cost, I'm sure. But whatever it was, several of the pods require more physical interactions."

As Chief Hernandez crested the stairs, he saw the similar mishmash of patched-together colors and textures of residential pods. Looking at the direction of the upstairs entrance, Chief Hernandez could see the layout of the stacked pods followed the same pattern as the one downstairs. Right up to the formation of pods that blocked the entrance.

"This way, Chief." Lady Desh guided Omar gently by the arm toward the back of El Corazon. They snaked their way through several rows of pods until they were all the way at the back of the block. Lady Desh pointed to the pod at the bottom of a three-pod stack in the dimmest corner.

A woman lay in the pod right above Lucia's, holding her stomach and groaning in pain. Lady Desh tended to the sick woman. A pitcher of water hung from some netting. She helped the woman drink.

"What's wrong with her?" Chief Hernandez asked.

"AIDS. She used to be a body artist. Private shows for the right price. She can't afford the medicine. We will be moving her later today so that Cynthia can care for her better."

Omar squatted down next to the lower pod. He looked at the flat section of the pod where the open button should've appeared. The panel stayed blank. Omar grabbed a knob at the center of Lucia's pod's shutter. Twisting the knob and thumbing its center button, he opened it. Inside was a meticulously clean pod with no modifications.

"How long was she living here?"

"She downsized to this pod about a year ago. Shortly after, she started her final year of graduate school."

"Hmm," Chief Hernandez grunted.

The pod's interior had been cleaned down to its original aluminum base. Whatever previous paint job was there had been removed long ago. All that was left were small color fragments still tucked tightly in the aluminum seams at the joints. A handmade hemp knitted laundry bag hung in one corner with a few articles of clothing in it. The chief reached out and squeezed it feeling only clothes. The foam mattress was covered in sheets neatly made with an old quilt folded at what would have been the foot of the bed. A rental tag on the sheets and quilt had a return date in two more months. There was no pillow.

Omar took a hit of wolfberry as he looked around the pod. He thumbed the button to one of the two storage compartments. A latch gave way, and the compartment dropped down, revealing neatly stacked jumpers of different colors strapped to the door. A handwritten list of clothes along with rental return dates for the articles was set on an old post-it note. Both outer and undergarments were plain. There was nothing that indicated a second, more seedy life. Chief Hernandez climbed into the pod to better examine its contents, leaving his boots to hang out of the pod. He reached over and turned the overhead light on.

"What are you looking for, Chief?"

"Anything."

Omar closed the compartment door and opened the other. Inside was a graduate cap and tassel, some small personal knickknacks, and a cheap personal hygiene kit. All photos or personal diary entries would be uploaded on Lucia's personal cloud. Omar mentally cussed himself out, realizing he had missed sending the request for Lucia's cloud. That he could quickly get from CENCOM. Omar leaned back and closed his eyes, opening his email app. He struggled to think up the words for the request. Omar opened his eyes so that his ocular video feed could read the pantomime keystrokes he needed to make for the request. Something caught his eye. He stared at the light panel above him. A small rectangular shadow blocked the stream of light from the other side of its plastic covering. Omar closed the email app.

Reaching up, he was able to push the cover to one side. He fumbled, and the rectangle shadow fell, landing on his chest. Looking at the little thing, Chief Hernandez slung his legs out of the pod and sat up.

"Hmm, this looks like one of my vaping cartridges. Did Lucia vape?"

"Chief, I think that's an old USB dongle."

"A dingle? What's it used for?"

"Dongle. Don-gull. They are used to store information."

"I should probably give it to the detectives, then." Chief Hernandez pocketed the dongle. Then, pulling himself up out of the pod, he turned to Lady Desh.

"Ready when you are."

"The garden I want to show is on our way. This garden has nothing unique compared to the other two, as Lucia improved all three. Still, you will get a good idea of what she was doing to improve our resources around here. Her nanobots have really helped to increase our harvest."

"I thought nanobots weren't very efficient when it came to plants. Where'd she get 'em?"

Lady Desh stopped and looked Omar in the eyes. "She coded them herself at State. Once she showed proof of concept, everyone in Alameda volunteered a small fraction of their own nanobots to be transformed. Don't you remember the drive we had last fall?"

Omar stopped to think when his phone rang.

[Sec.Off.J.WRIGHT]: Chief, you better get back here. The coroner wouldn't wait and immediately picked up the body per CENCOM's orders.

[Chief.Sec.O.HERNANDEZ]: Have the detectives shown up yet?

[Sec.Off.J.WRIGHT]: They passed the coroner as they came in. The woman looks to be spitting mad.

[Chief.Sec.O.HERNANDEZ]: All right. I'm on my way.

"I need to get back to Carousel Way. There are a couple of dicks that want to yell at me." He tried again to open the app and send the request for Lucia's cloud. This time he was able to think up the words. He quickly thought up and sent the email through his mind's eye.

"I sent a request to check out Lucia's cloud storage. If you think of anything, could you keep me posted, Lady Desh?"

"When's the last time you saw any of the gardens, Chief Hernandez?"

"It's been a couple of years. Not since Mr. Johnson was found to have passed away from that stroke. There's no need to check them out when there's never a call to them. The byway keeps me busy enough."

"Please stop by on your way to Carousel Way. Lucia was doing remarkable work. The kind that increased our food output threefold."

"I will. Sorry, I don't have much to tell you. Maybe after I speak with the detectives, we'll get a better idea of what happened."

"Chief, it's strange to have a security code on a dropped stream and not a maintenance code, isn't it?"

"They do come up from time to time but for a death? Yeah, it's pretty strange. Thank you for your time and the breakfast, Lady Desh."

Omar headed back out of El Corazon through the second-floor exit. Mournful murmurs emanated through the tight corridors of the pods as he passed. Then, stepping out onto the byway, he again felt a shift in tone and tune among the inhabitants.

Chief Hernandez made his way over to the stairs nearest to Carousel Way. He took a hit from his vape before reentering the fray. By now, the byway was packed with daily goings-on. Lucia's death had brought a good portion of layabouts out to linger around the scene of the crime. Carousel Way was crowded. He could hear yelling as soon as he had left El Corazon. Descending the stairs, Chief Hernandez could see poor Johnny getting a face full of hate. Detective De La Torre was very petite for a cop. Her diamond-shaped head rocketed back and forth like a chicken pecking at the ground as she laid into Security Officer Johnny. Even standing a full foot shorter than Johnny, her verbal assault made him look small. Her partner seemed nonplussed about the exchange. There was something about how her partner stood next to her. Her partner rolled back his shoulders, adjusting his own posture ever so slightly. In a manner Omar had seen all too often, he watched the man's lat flex then relax.

Omar stopped in his tracks and gasped as he realized who Detective De La Torre's partner was. His heart skipped a beat. Detective Jack Williams was a tall, broad-shouldered, brutish-looking man with sandy blond hair neatly oiled and combed. He parted his hair on the right side. The detective wore a crisp white military-pressed shirt and solid, dark forest green tie. Matching green trousers had been just as sharply pressed as his shirt. Both Jack's badge and his gun hung from the detective's belt. A beige sun trench coat hung over his right arm.

Omar hadn't seen his former partner since they split years ago. Not wanting to feel anything more than the initial shock,

Omar decided to focus on the task at hand. Rescuing his second from the verbal assault.

He announced his approach. "All right! I'm here. Lay off my officer already," Omar bellowed above the crowd, which parted.

With Detective De La Torre's verbal assault abated, she stood still, smoldering at Omar as he made his way closer.

Omar took one more hit to steady his nerves before dealing with the detective. *Beep.* He mindlessly switched out the cartridge while he made his way through the crowd. Alameda residents slapped him on the back as he passed.

"What's the big idea, digging into my man, Detective?"

"Boy, you got a lot of nerve, Chief. I told you not to move a hair. And what the fuck do I see walking in, but the goddamn coroner on his way out with the victim!"

Chief Hernandez raised his hand.

"I'm sorry. That wasn't Johnny's call. It was mine. The coroner was only supposed to pick the body up if you couldn't get here before it got too hot. CENCOM had other plans, apparently. Sped up the process. Again, I'm sorry."

The detective slowed her roll but was still visibly annoyed.

"Yeah. We would have gotten here sooner, but there was a holdup getting authorization to come down here. You look like shit, Omar. How you been?" Detective Jack Williams asked as he offered his hand and a smile to Omar.

"Hi, Jack." Omar took his hand, releasing quickly before turning to the crowd. Omar felt his cheeks flush.

"All right, everyone, show's over. Get back to your day. Bo. Murrey. Start getting this crowd out of here." Omar gestured to the two other security guards to keep the crowd back.

"Johnny, did you get the bio-sweep?"

"Yes, Chief."

"Go ahead and transmit it to the detective here."

"Yes, sir."

"I have something for you as well, Detective. I found this in Lucia's pod. I'm told that it's some kind of outdated information storage device." Omar handed over the dongle. "Peace?"

The detective pocketed it without taking her eyes off Omar. "All right. For now. But this whole thing stinks."

"Well then, you're not going to like this," Jack said.

"Yeah, what's that?" Detective De La Torre turned to her partner.

"The file that kid sent over is corrupted. We have no scan."

And like that, Detective De La Torre was right back to losing her shit with Omar. It was sometime around her proclamation to "put her boot up his ass" and "his ancestors spitting out the laces" that Omar thought, overdosing on wolfberry wouldn't be the worst way to go right about now. He tried to take a hit. Nothing came out. He tried to pull the cartridge out, but it seemed to be lodged in pretty good.

"Shit," Omar said out loud.

"Shit?! Shit, what? You got something to say, Chief?" Detective De La Torre stretched out the word "chief" with as much condescension she could muster.

"No. I was just commenting on my vape not working."

"Your vape not working? Your fucking vape not working? Are you kidding me? We have a dead girl—no crime scene evidence, no video stream—and you are more concerned with your vape? Chief, you're fucking disgusting."

Omar had enough. He squared his shoulders and leaned in.

"That's Master Detective Hernandez, Detective. I don't know what kind of holy terror you think you are trying to pull off here, but I would have bounced your loud mouth down to patrol where you fucking belong. Wah, my crime scene. Nut the fuck up and do your fucking job. When I was on the Force, we didn't have this level of augmented coverage, and we still got our man. You fucking drip."

"And look at you now, you fucking junkie."

"Fucking junkie? Did you figure that out with your keen detective superpowers, you dirty cocksucker? Get the fuck out of my mall." Omar pointed at the door. Detective De La Torre, thinking he meant to push her, reached out and grabbed his arm. Muscle memory kicked in, and Chief Hernandez reversed the move and knocked the detective back. Detective Jack Williams and Johnny jumped in between them. The crowd that formed started to jeer.

"Okay, Omar. That's enough," Jack said.

"Keep your dog on a leash then, Jack." Omar turned around to walk away. "Johnny, see what happened with the scan and try to resend it to the detective. If that doesn't work, rescan the area." He tried to take a hit from his vape one more time—still nothing.

Omar sent a text to his dealer.

"Forget it," Jack added. "Update from HQ. All resources are pulled. No further action is to be taken on the case."

"Disgusting," Detective De La Torre spat out. "What, Hernandez? Did you have a buddy in corporate take care of it for you?"

"Huh? Don't let the door hit you on your way out."

As the detectives made their way over to the door, Jack turned around, looked back at Omar, and shrugged, allowing his back to open the door to the sun-blasted outside.

"Nice seeing you, Omar," Jack said with a grin.

Chief Hernandez nodded in reply. Omar looked around. The crowd was still there.

"All right. You need to get your gratuitous violence fix somewhere else. Let's move."

The crowd began to disperse.

"Hey, Johnny?"

"Yes, Chief?"

"Get me that scan, anyway. They may have had all their resources pulled, but I'm not done. Not yet, at least. Have you ever dealt with the Force before?"

"That was my first, sir."

"Well, don't let her dictate what you think they're like. Okay? Most of the Force are good guys like Jack there. You know, Johnny, you may have just joined the team a little while ago, but from what I've seen, you could go work for the Force. You'd do a whole lot better than Detective De La Torre."

Johnny looked at Omar and smiled. "She really got under your skin, huh? No, Chief, I'm okay with the path I'm on."

"Well, if you ever change your mind, I can get Williams to put in a good word for you. I've seen you with the residents. You listen to them and keep things calm."

"You knew Detective Williams before?" Johnny asked.

"Yeah, he was my partner once upon a time. My special talent was getting us in trouble. His was getting us out. He's saved my ass more times than I like to remember. The law was a lot looser back then, but there was a code you had to follow. We looked out for each other."

"What happened?"

"I pushed things too far one too many times, and we had to split up, so I didn't drag him down with me." Omar went to take a hit from his vape. "Ahh, shit. I have to run a quick errand, Johnny. Then I might swing over to the gardens if you need me for anything."

"All right, Chief."

Omar walked away from the crime scene back down the fairway, making a right down a short corridor. Like the rest of the living facility, pods lay along the wall. Still, here and there, Omar could see the walls of the corridor were painted in black-and-white movie characters from the previous millennium. Old electric neon tube lighting hung limply from the ceiling's faux awning that guided him towards the exit and tunnel that led to the old movie theater next to Alameda.

The tunnel that connected Alameda to the theater was added years after both were initially built. It was designed to protect large volumes of foot traffic from the harsh valley sun. Omar's lonely footfalls on the terracotta tile flooring echoed up and down the hall, adding to the sense of isolation. The mismatched architecture gave a disjointed sense to those traversing the path. Lights went from dim to bright back to dim again with no windows to gaze upon the outside world. The accompanying hum from the lights waxed and waned as he walked closer or farther from each working light. The tunnel had a high arched ceiling. Graffiti covered the walls up to a certain point, with no pods lining the walls to obscure the artist's intent. Murals from the collapse of the old union, intertwined with slogans of patriotism like "Better dead than Red," "Freedoms just another word for nothing left to lose," and "Join or Die." Names of street artists were crossed out and overwritten. Layers and layers that resulted in a kaleidoscope of expression. Markers by people that want to proclaim, "I was here. I mattered."

The closer Chief Hernandez got to the theater, the colder he felt. The theater still had a functioning air conditioning unit that fed part of the tunnel. Walking through the glass push doors into the theater felt like stepping into a walk-in refrigerator.

It was simultaneously refreshing as well as unsettling. Omar was bathed in the purple hue of neon from the blue and red lighting that ran the length of the theater's ceiling. Pods once again filled the room four high. There was enough room for a narrow trail that led to the ticket counter/concessions register.

The theater was leased from CENCOM by an eccentric old hipster called the Usher. The Usher believed that movies could only really be experienced sitting in a packed room, viewed through your own eyes.

To Omar, there was something voyeuristic in the viewings. Like he was invading someone's personal space. Regardless, the eccentric old hipster was his dealer. He caught a movie once a week.

To help ease the cost of the lease, the Usher kept most of the theater's space for pods. Some pods were dens of pleasure for those requiring unique company. Only one theater was used for its intended purpose. The Usher made fresh popcorn each day, filling the lobby with the unmistakable aroma. Omar thought about what it would be like living in a pod that constantly had the chemical smell of synth butter. The large room had a glass wall to the south for admission. It was covered with aluminum foil, cardboard, or simple sheets of thin pulp paper to try to keep the sun out. Several doors were covered with plywood and chained or bolted closed, except for a guarded single-entry point.

Omar made his way up to the counter and chimed the augmented bell resting there. He leaned on the counter, resting his back against it, and looked over the pods. Several of the inhabitants were milling about, but it looked like most of the pods were closed and sealed. After a while, an elderly man came around the corner and walked behind the counter. The

Usher was taller than most, with long gray hair past his shoulders. His height seemed to weigh on him, causing the old man to slump over like a very long question mark. He had a beaked nose that rested on a thin scruffy beard. Blood red lips emerged from the white of his facial hair. The old man wore threadbare brown coveralls, which hung loosely from his shoulders.

"What's showing, old-timer?" Omar asked.

"How do you do, Chief? We're having a Keanu Reeves marathon this week. Right now, it is *Johnny Mnemonic*."

"Is it any good?"

"Dina Meyer is smoking hot in it, with an amazing cast."

"Who's Dina Meyer?"

"Don't be an ignoramus, Chief. Fucking google her. You won't regret it. You know it was one of Congressman Rollins' earlier films."

"Yeah, I noticed you didn't say whether it was any good," Omar said.

"Can I offer you any concessions?"

"Didn't you get my text?"

"No. The only thing I'm letting through is the counter chime. You need something?" the Usher asked.

"Yes."

Omar pulled out his vape along with all the empty cartridges he had on him. Placing them on the counter, he slid them across.

"The vape stopped working just a little bit ago. The carts just don't seem to last as long with a full battery. Two fucking hits. Really?"

"I might have gotten some bad doses. I'll take a look. Anything else? No? Here, take this loaner. So you can enjoy the movie."

The old dealer slid over a smaller vape with Omar's weekly supply of new carts. Omar picked it up and took a long pull, letting out a billowing cloud of purple. He heard the familiar chime of his account as the price of the doses appeared in his HUD. The chime echoed through a remote cave that gently bounced off the waters of Omar's mind. His shoulders relaxed.

"Wow. Good shit."

"Least I can do for the cart issue. I'm not billing you full price for the better shit."

"Thanks, man. And the repairs?" Omar asked.

"I'll hit you up after I figure out what's wrong."

Omar took another hit.

"Hey, you're going to want to take it easy with that."

"All right, thanks. Hey, text me when you get to the *John Wick* shit, man."

"Sure thing, Chief."

"You mind if I sit in the theater while I get my head straight?"

"It's all good, Chief. If you actually sit through a whole movie, though, I'll auto-charge you, okay?"

"I won't be here long enough for that."

"Sure."

"What's this shit called?" Omar held up the vape before taking another hit.

"Nighthowler," the Usher said with a pirate's grin.

Omar floated down the same hallway the old man had come from. The hallway to the theater was like the lobby and like almost every inch of Alameda, lined with pods. Which now seemed to shine brightly. Fractals of neon light danced before him. Omar smiled to himself. All but one of the sixteen movie screens had been converted to housing or storage. The only room to show old-fashioned movies was closest to the lobby. It still had two pairs of pods on either side of its entrance. When he walked into the theater, he stopped to allow his eyes to adjust to the darkness. Omar's HUD brought up an outline of his surroundings to help guide him. An overlay of red wire framed the aisle and walls. The tiny red wires became frayed, wobbled, and melted into new shapes as Omar tried to ascend the stairs to a seat. The theater was practically empty, with a handful of junkies scattered around the room. All dosing different shit, flying on different trips.

The best part about hacking the nanobots was that coders could write all kinds of different vape experiences. Euphoric, uppers, downers, ecstasy, psychedelic, even religious for those rare few who still believed. Hacking nanobots was highly illegal. It broke all sorts of warranties. No one ever enforced it since vaping was required to enjoy a beer. Prices were based on the cleanliness of the code. There were stories abound of top-shelf coders buying private islands. Omar didn't know how it went from code to a liquid state, and he didn't care. Just so long as it worked when he took a hit.

Carefully, he made his way up the stairs to find a suitable seat. When he spotted a decent perch, he crashed into the seat. Staring at the giant projection in front of him, he took another hit. Keanu was on screen, proclaiming something about room service.

"Huh, I prefer it when he plays a cop," he whispered to no one in particular as he let out another large cloud. Omar felt his eyes get heavy. He looked down at the vape in his hand.

"What the fuck?" he mumbled.

Clutching it tightly to not drop it in his loose fingers, he crammed it into his pocket.

The play actors on screen seemed to slip and slide into the same cavern his HUD chime played in.

Shit. I took too much, he thought, trying to turn it around.

Omar closed his eyes.

Omar found himself strolling through dry soil. Footfalls crushed the leaves of grass that grew, dried, and died sporadically through the land. Heatwaves created a continuous mirage of distant lakes at the foot of faraway red clay hand-molded mountains. He sensed a dryness in him and looked up as the rain began to fall. The drops dived down to the earth, crashing in an explosion of deep blues and turquoise. They were simultaneously large and small. Here, yet distant.

Omar still felt dry. Lifting his head to the cloudless sky, he opened his mouth to the rainfall in an attempt to quench his thirst. No drops fell on his face. He reached out his hands in cups to catch the delicate moisture. Each time he was close to one landing in his palm, it seemed to shift at the last moment, continuing to crash in the dry pebble-ridden land.

The deep blue droplets made small pools of water. Omar fell to his knees and crawled to the nearest one. Plunging his hands into the cool pond, Omar recoiled at the sight of the lifeless face of Lucia peering back at him. Her mouth opened, and crystalline crustaceans scuttled out. Hastily, Omar tried to pull away, falling back on his ass. Omar looked around while he felt the hot, dry pebbles of the wasteland under his hands. Puddles, ponds, and streams formed and dissolved all around him from the blue drops. The turquoise droplets seemed to form small plants that quickly sprouted out of the land, withered, and died. Bearing his fear, he crawled forward to another pool. He felt the weight of the rain on his back. The shower was transforming into a storm now, picking up momentum. Omar felt its desire to develop into a full tempest. Pummeling him, beating him into the ground. Each drop was getting heavier, to where he almost couldn't bear it. Still, he ached with dryness.

Panic rose inside Omar as he looked for shelter. Stumbling to his feet, he ran for the nearest mountains. The breast-shaped monolith in the distance called to him. Looking back behind him, he saw each step left was tarred compared to the tan, dry soil. The rain recoiled from the tar prints. As sticky tentacles of death formed, the tar reached out, connecting with one another, like bonding neurons. It grew. The black liquid chains rose off the ground and began wrapping themselves with each other.

Omar felt its sentience. He quickened his pace, fighting the storm's ferocity and terror of the growing unknown. Before him, he saw Lady Desh calling for him. Her nakedness felt foreign and obscene in contrast to their surroundings.

He ran towards her as dread began to climb inside him. A massive, fully formed serpent lingered over him. With each step, Omar pushed forward. The serpent was rising to its full height. The rain washed away the sludge from which it had emerged, showing the faces Omar often dreamed about, glistening like scales on the snake. The faces, twisted with pain, quietly screamed in agony from beneath the surface. It struck out to devour him. Just as he was consumed, Omar looked back to the Lady Desh, who had turned her back on him.

Omar awoke with a start, kicking the chair in front of him.

"Shh," came out from somewhere in the theater.

"Sorry."

Omar got up and made his way down the stairs. He looked at the screen. A man with gray hair was standing next to a small half-naked child. The child was wearing a cowboy hat and holstered revolvers. It looked like the man was speaking to his wife.

"You know I could put this on later…" said the gray-haired man.

Omar's legs were stiff, and his body ached from sleeping in the chair. Halfway down the stairs, his legs turned to Jell-O, and he gripped the handrail. He tried to shake the fog from his limbs.

The Usher was sitting in one of the front-row seats. When he noticed Omar struggling down the stairs, he hopped up and helped him out of the theater. As soon as they were out in the lobby, Omar turned on him.

"What the fuck, man? What was in that shit?"

"Nighthowler, Chief. I told you to take it easy."

"Fuck. I needed to get my head on straight, not go on a mission."

"I'm sorry, bro. I didn't mean for you to get lost. We cool?"

Still shaking the cobwebs out of his skull, Omar looked at the old pusher, who wore a face of concern. The theater was technically outside the Tribunal's oversight which meant he answered to Omar to keep his residence. Omar exhaled and wiped the last of the nightmare from his eyes.

"Yeah, you fucking degenerate. We're cool."

"Thanks."

"What was wrong with my gear?" Omar asked.

"You had this doohickey crammed in where a cartridge is supposed to go."

Omar recognized what the Usher had and snatched the drive from the old man's hands, dropping it in the back pockets of his trousers, hoping it didn't register on any of the cameras.

"Thanks."

The Usher handed Omar back his vape. Omar checked to make sure his wolfberry was back in and not any more of that nighthowler. He took a hit, pocketed his vape, and pulled the loaner back out. Omar ejected the nighthowler. Instead of putting the rest of the nighthowler in his front trouser pockets, he put it in his breast pocket.

"So, you liked the nighthowler?" the Usher asked.

"Yes, but not in the middle of the day. How much do I owe you?"

"Twenty for the repairs and fifty for the three movies."

"Three movies?"

"Yeah, you sat through *The Lake House*, *A Scanner Darkly*, and *My Own Private Idaho*."

"Are you fucking kidding me? You slip me a fucking roofie and expect me to pay you for three movies?"

"Well, I mean, I told you to be careful. It's a free country, and you're a big boy. I figured you could handle your shit. But if you want to be a little bitch about it, I guess I'll only charge you for one."

"Here's your seventy. Give me a beer. What's the name of that movie I was watching?"

"*Parenthood*. It was one of Reeves's first films."

The Usher set down a beer bottle, and the familiar sound of coins chimed. Omar picked up the beer and took a pull.

"If it was one of the first ones, what kind of order are you playing these things in?"

"Autobiographical."

"Autobio—who runs a theater and plays a series like that? Your customers don't want to watch it in that order."

"Shit, Omar. My customers aren't in there for the movie."

Omar took another long pull from the beer and headed to the restroom. The hand-stained door squeaked as he pushed through. Omar's boots thudded dully as he made his way to an open stall. He set his beer down on the toilet paper dispenser, squatted, and went to work.

Sitting in the stall, Omar took another long pull of the wolfberry, trying to burn away the dope aftereffects of the nighthowler. He chased it with a swallow of beer before exhaling and went through his messages. He waited for his body to decide whether it would pass anything. For whatever reason, sometimes wolfberry caused constipation. Today Omar felt backed up.

The first message he got was a response to the request to access cloud storage.

CENCOM INC.

ACCESS REQUEST
CLOUD STORAGE
MALL HOUSING FACILITY
LOCATION: CA 93726
FACILITY #3-03452978224
OCCUPANT: VITORES, LUCIA M.
OCCUPATION: STUDENT
STATUS: DECEASED
REQUESTED BY: CHIEF HERNANDEZ, O.

CENCOM INC. regrets to inform Chief Hernandez that access is denied due to copyright laws. Deceased occupant Lucia M. Vitores's cloud storage is the sole property of FSUR&D Inc.

END REPORT

Omar focused on FSUR&D Inc. until his HUD brought up a definition. FSUR&D Inc. was the research arm of the university where Lucia had been conducting her doctoral research. Omar rubbed his head as he took another long pull from his beer.

Whole goddamn thing just keeps getting harder and harder, he thought. He typed up a request to the university for access before moving on to his following message.

The next message was denying his request to stay the deletion of the stored footage. The reason was the same code he read from the initial report. He brought up another message, trying to distract himself from the bowel movement.

CENCOM INC.
CODE INDEX: [sec7-58426-265a]

REQUESTED BY: CHIEF HERNANDEZ, O.

[sec7-58426-265a]: Classified due to executive interest.

END REPORT

For fuck's sake. Omar was beginning to get annoyed. This was a lot of bullshit for a local.

Omar's stomach began to cramp, and he leaned forward. Uncontrollably, his body vacated what it had held on to. Omar didn't feel the shit so much as he rode what seemed like a never-ending splash of liquid. Beads of sweat formed on his brow. He closed his eyes, trying to relax, only to have the perpetual HUD in his view. Annoying. Intrusive. *We all need to get our heads examined*, he thought. A text dinged.

[Sec.Off.J.WRIGHT]: Where are you?

[Chief.Sec.O.HERNANDEZ]: Bathroom. What's up?

[Sec.Off.J.WRIGHT]: You're going to be late for the funeral. Lady Desh is expecting you.

Omar went back to his messages and found one he had overlooked. Lady Desh had sent him a formal request to come to the funeral and participate in the ceremony.

[Chief.Sec.O.HERNANDEZ]: On my way. How much time do I have?

[Sec.Off.J.WRIGHT]: 10, maybe less.

Omar hit the first seashell that sprayed down his ass with a liquid cleaner. The second seashell blasted everything down with an intense stream of air. Omar went back and forth between the two features. Finally, when he felt clean, he pressed the third and final seashell that dosed him with a powdered deodorizer and perfume.

He stood up and quickly buckled his pants on as he hastily grabbed his beer and headed out the stall.

Omar gave the Usher a half-hearted wave as he headed for the tunnel at a light jog, not wanting to shake up his beer. Ultimately, he stopped at a trash bin, pounded the rest, and tossed the bottle. Hands free, he ran full-sprint for his apartment.

Omar started undoing buttons before he was even through the door. Stripping as fast as he could, he reached in and pulled his dress uniform, still in its protective plastic from when it was issued years earlier. Chief Hernandez ran his hand over his face, cursing the decision not to shave that morning. Stopping everything, he ran over to the refresher and fired up his electric razor. While working over his face with the razor, Omar walked over and checked his personal fridge for a beer. He checked himself in the mirror before continuing to get dressed, alternating between hitting his wolfberry and swigging a fresh beer.

Chief Hernandez had never put on the dress uniform before. It was oversized and baggy on him. It came with a hat that rested so low he couldn't see straight. Omar tossed it back in his closet and started transferring the content of his pockets from his pants to the slacks. He decided to keep it light. Most of the wolfberry he had picked up went in a small yellow box that rested next to his bed. The nighthowler he decided to put in the closet and save for a special occasion. He pulled the USB dongle out of his pocket and looked at it. He tossed it on the table before slipping his shoes on and heading for the door.

Omar stopped. The door cracked open. Feeling both rushed and that he was forgetting something, he looked over his shoulder. Not able to leave. He walked back to the pile of clothes on his bed, reached down, and pulled off the black armband he had been wearing all day.

That wasn't it, he thought.

Finally, he convinced himself to pick up the dongle. He slowly walked across the room, looking at the dongle the whole time. Chief Hernandez pocketed it, making sure not to put it in the same pocket as his wolfberry cart. Only then did Omar feel his feet had the strength to hurry to the funeral.

Omar followed the traffic of residents, stopping only once to throw up some beer that had been sloshing in his gut. He grumbled to himself that he should have stopped to grab a bite before. *Maybe after the memorial service*, he thought. The funeral was held just outside Garden Two. Garden Two was considered the principal garden of the three as it was near the center of Alameda. When Alameda had been a mall, Garden Two had been a simple entrance walkway on the west side. It had only two small stores in it. Large windows overhead instead of plaster for a ceiling, filling the space with all the sunshine it needed to grow food. Now it housed vertical gardens that climbed all the way up on a rotating automated system, and solar panels dispersed throughout. The panels were anywhere the plants couldn't fit to grow. Just outside the garden, a stage had been erected for the funeral.

By the time Omar made it outside of Garden Two, a sea of somber attendees was so densely packed together he couldn't get closer than thirty feet to the dais. The Tribunal and other residence-like store managers sat on the stage, waiting for the funeral to begin. The crowd was a sea of tears and sorrow so intense that one couldn't help but feel remorse with the others. Omar tried to stoically tuck in his lip and fought against the urge to cry. An augmented reality button hung in the air over the crowd. Omar clicked it, and a ceremony program came up in his HUD. He focused on that and his vape to help against feeling too much. The whole ordeal seemed short. Only one speaker and one song.

Everything was covered in white. The walls had sheets draping down. A small stage had been erected and covered in white bunting and flowers. On the right of the stage were the white fold-out chairs filled with Alameda's dignitaries and a small podium. The podium was also dressed in white, with a wreath of white roses that adorned the face. A single blue rose rested at the base of the white wreath. All of the seats were filled except one—the fourth seat after the Tribunal before a collection of shop owners. Omar got a sense that it was meant for him. Standing on the far left of the stage was a small but clear picture of Lucia. Lucia was wearing bright green coveralls, sitting beside a plant, smiling. Her gloved hands held a small shovel and were covered in soil. CENCOM's copyright glyph watermarked the entire bottom third of the picture.

With the entrance bathed in early evening light through the greenery. Lucia's smile seemed to shine even brighter.

In the center of the stage was a sizable fold-out table also covered in a white sheet. Flowers adorned every inch of the stage. Mostly the fake cloth flowers but some real white roses as well. There were so many flowers that they were piled in heaps at the feet of the table, turning it into a bed of flowers. Chief Hernandez noticed no customary urn resting in the center of the table.

It was unheard of for anyone to be buried. There were no more funeral plots to rest in. No more land to be zoned for the dead. Legally, everyone was expected to be processed for recycling. Healthy organs were removed for high-end transplants and the rest of the remains were cremated. Should anyone care, a person's ashes were put in a basic aluminum urn. Once the coroner cleared the body, the process took only a couple of hours. Lucia wouldn't have been worth a full postmortem. By now, if Alameda was having a service, her urn should be up on stage. There was none.

Fritz saddled up next to Omar.

"Where you coming from?" Omar asked.

"I was five people away, Chief."

"Oh."

"I think you're supposed to be on stage?"

"I'll give you one hundred bucks if you can make that happen, buddy."

Fritz looked around at the tight-knit group blocking the stage. "Yeah. Good luck with that."

Chief Hernandez looked at Fritz, and he had an idea. "Maybe you can help me with something else."

"Oh, yeah. What?"

The chief stared Fritz in the eyes, holding his gaze. He palmed the dongle and handed it discreetly to Fritz. Omar tried to remember the phrase he had heard once in passing.

"The elevator always seems to be broken. Which is why I always take the escalator."

Fritz let out a snort. "I think you mean stairs. Try using the stairs next time." Fritz pocketed the dongle without looking at it.

"Did you know they're livestreaming this, Chief?"

Omar looked at Fritz, perplexed.

Fritz continued, "Yeah. Lady Desh's idea."

"Why would she want to do that?"

"She said it was to show the rest of the world what it is like living in CENCOM's ghetto."

"Is it working?"

"Twenty-six million views and climbing."

"So, no. Not even scratched the surface."

"My guess is most of those views are either other ghettos or people fixated on the macabre. Still, it is climbing. You never know."

"Yeah, right. Text me if it clears half a bill, then we'll talk." Chief Hernandez looked around one more time. "I hope you can see 'cause neither of us is going anywhere." Omar tried to text Johnny to see if he could make it to the stage in his place. Someone from his department should be up there warming the seat. Nothing.

"Man, I think I really fucked up."

"Yeah, but you tried."

"Let's hope the Sponsors feel that way." Omar took a hit from his vape.

The murmuring in the crowd picked up, and both men tracked the source to the stage. Grandfather Sandoval had stood and made the short journey to the podium.

Grandfather Sandoval, or simply Grandfather to most residents, was the oldest of the Tribunal and head of the Pueblo community. The Pueblo was the smallest of all the communities but the wealthiest, structured as one large family arranged around a complex polygamous marriage system. Although Grandfather was the official Sponsor of the community, he had four wives referred to as the Grandmothers. Grandfather's original wife and his one true love had passed years ago. These wives were joined to him in contractual name alone. Although Omar had heard one of them was sweet on Grandfather and doted over him, which Grandmother was a clan secret. Grandmother was a title of great authority in the Pueblo community. Husbands and wives that were to marry into the community had to get the blessing from the Grandmothers. Interviews were held in private, and approved marriage expectations were that the family's growth was beneficial to all economically. Spouse swapping was common but required at least one Grandmother to give her blessing. All spouses were involved in rearing the children. Of course, some were more natural at it than others. Divorce was allowed with a renouncement of all claims to the property since the property was looked at as belonging to and remaining with the family. Divorce didn't happen often.

When a child born in the community came of age, their property was held separate until they decided to marry into the family. If they decided to leave, the young adult kept what belonged to them and left. To Omar's understanding, marriage was strictly a choice. The Grandmothers did not want anyone marrying into the family that did not want to be there, which also meant that growing up in Pueblo did not guarantee marriage. Exclusion from the family happened less than divorce, but it did happen. There was no drug use. Teen pregnancies were unheard of. And Pueblo had the highest employment rate of any community in Alameda.

As complex as their community was, whatever they were doing, they were doing it right as far as Omar was concerned. He was never called in to assist.

The Grandmothers ran the day-to-day operations of Pueblo, which allowed Grandfather to tend to the gardens. For years he struggled to get help other than Pueblo members, operating the three gardens with a meager crew. Grandfather would spend his days worrying the gardens would be lost upon his passing. Until the day that Lucia had started to assist him. She brought with her an army of young residents to help, and with her guidance, the gardens flourished. So richly had the gardens grown that Alameda grew more produce than they bought for the first time ever. Easing the accumulation of debt that many residents accrued simply trying to feed themselves. This, in turn, encouraged even more residents to help at the gardens. The fear that once gripped Grandfather was replaced with joy.

"Friends and loved ones of Lucia, could you please part so that the deceased can make her way to the stand?" Omar heard Grandfather weep through the speaker in his ear. The tiny audio device helped the soft, tear-filled voice of the elder carry over the audience.

And as if Omar wasn't miserable enough, mourners directly in front of him started stepping back, forcing him into those gathered behind him. Lucia and the pallbearers emerged from a storefront opposite the stage to Omar's right. The mourners pushed into Omar as the crowd tried to open a path. He gasped at the sight.

Six men dressed all in white except for a single blue rose pinned to their lapels carried a bed of white flowers. The men's faces were covered in a white veil similar to Lady Desh's black veil. Omar couldn't make out who they were. Resting on top, wrapped in fine white cloth linen, was Lucia. Every inch of her was wrapped like a mummy with a transparent white cover over her face, so you could see it was her. A drone flew above her, recording her lifeless body gliding across the crowd. A new button appeared, and Omar clicked it. A small video showed up in his HUD and streamed the feed. She looked to be resting, lovely and at peace—a stark contrast to how Omar had seen her last. Her arms were folded on her breast, hands grasping a single blue rose. The rose stood out, drawing Omar's attention to the spot. A banner lay under the rose with calligraphy text written in blue ink. It read, "Freedom's just another word for nothing left to lose." Women and men started to cry and wail. It was too much. Omar closed the feed.

As the procession passed, hands would raise and reach out, attempting to touch a foot or leg of the deceased. White flowers of various types were tossed upon the bed. Mounds of flowers grew to the point that a flower tossed would simply tumble back to the ground. Still, they were tossed.

"My god!" Omar couldn't help but blurt out, awestruck by the sight.

"I've never seen anything like this," Fritz let out.

"Where are all these flowers coming from?" Omar asked.

"That would be the Lady," Fritz explained. "She said it was important to remember the brightest of us. To honor how much she gave back to the community. Her exact words were, 'Lucia deserved more than a pauper's funeral.' All of this she has paid for out of pocket. But I didn't expect this."

The pallbearers carried their charge to the stage, leaving cascading flowers and a wake of people eager to close the gap. Slowly, the pallbearers took the stage, cautiously climbing the steep incline so Lucia would not slip from her perch. Lose flowers rained down on the attendants. After laying her to rest on the makeshift dais, each of the pallbearers knelt, not leaving their post. It was then that Omar noticed they were armed. Each bearer had a holstered handgun inside their coat breast. Gun ownership was contractually forbidden inside Alameda. Anyone found to own a firearm could face severe consequences, including being exiled and/or permanently banned from any of CENCOM's facilities. In the Central Valley, that led to too few choices for anyone to take the risk. It was the reason Omar didn't habitually carry his gun. Uncomfortably, Omar realized he would have to speak to Lady Desh about it.

Why did she add guns to the ceremony? Chief Hernandez thought. He shot Lady Desh a text and received an out of office reply.

Lady Desh slowly scanned the audience. She stopped when it looked like she was staring in Chief Hernandez's direction. Omar wasn't sure if she was staring at him, but he felt her gaze in his mind.

Grandfather Sandoval stood by the podium during all of this. He wiped his eyes with a tissue, collecting himself. After a moment, he continued. "Let us pray."

A wave of heads bowed, and Omar saw the drone leave its holding pattern of filming Lucia.

"God almighty, we humbly return to you one of your brightest. We thank you for sending us such a wonderful and beautiful example of your blessing. We thank you for-f-for the garden she has lovingly shared with us. Th-th-the time she has spent building and strengthening our communities. We ask that you embrace her and love her as we have. We ask that you help ease our loss and grant us the strength and hope to continue what she started. Amen."

"Amen," the crowd returned.

"Now, Lucia's Sponsor, Lady Desh, will share a few words."

Lady Desh stood up and floated to the podium, stopping only to embrace Grandfather. As Grandfather's words were soft and sorrowful, requiring assistance, Lady Desh's voice was clear and carried with little effort.

"And here we are. Once again, once more gathered to grieve for one of our own. It's not just one of us, though, is it? But the best of us. The one we all thought would carry us out of this misery. Lucia wasn't just another cog, another shlep to move the machine. Lucia was a guiding light that elevated Alameda. She believed, as do I, that our limitations were self-imposed. Intellect is not bound by wealth. Anything is possible if one simply puts their mind to it. And so, Lucia did. And she did extraordinary things. When the universe took her family away from her, she found a new family in Alameda. When children in her community needed tools to learn, she found them. And she worked hard to reach out to find the programs and equipment to help each of them grow. Lucia believed only the educated are truly free, spending her time teaching and tutoring those children herself, all while attending a university and working toward a doctorate. The only member of Alameda's family to ever achieve such a lofty academic height. Lucia's doctorate was not in education, although she would have done fine as an educator. As a programmable biologist focused on botany, she began to truly shape the world.

"You see, Lucia wanted to nourish us all. She cultivated the gardens of Alameda, working towards the Mars problem. How can mankind feed itself in such harsh conditions? Well, Lucia found an answer. In Alameda's gardens, we have crops the likes of which the world has not seen in some time. So much food that now, for the first time in Alameda's history, we can feed ourselves without incurring lifelong debt to a corporation, a debt that has kept us in bondage, a debt that has made slaves of us all. Lucia has figured out a way to not only free every man, woman, and child of Alameda but every man, woman, and child in all the Alamedas across the nation. Lucia did not secret these means of freedom away, by hiding them away so only she could turn a profit. She was working to share with the world. To guide mankind back from the desert to the promised land. She sprang up from the dried desert lands, a flower, a lone rose in the twisted, gnarled landscape, a beacon to all of us that life can persist even in the harshest climates.

"And they stepped on her for it. They crushed her, trying to snuff out our hopes and our dreams. But that which grows in a desert grows strong, and you cannot silence hope once sprung to life. You cannot hide from it. You must stand up to those who would try to extinguish hope. Remember, freedom's just another word for nothing left to lose. You, Alameda, and all the Alamedas around the country must carry Lucia's promise. We must no longer hide behind these walls under the yolk of servitude behind the veil of CENCOM's lies!"

Lady Desh removed the veil she had worn for as long as anyone in Alameda had known her. Lady Desh had not one scar on her face. She had aged since anyone had seen her without the veil. But it was her. Lady Desh. Not an augmented reality version that was overlaid with a computer-generated likeness, used by so many starlets. She presented to them all how the universe made her. But aging had made her so much more—more beautiful, more elegant, more formidable.

Even with tears running down her face, she radiated determination. Omar felt as if his eyes had stolen something. He had committed a blaspheme yet could not look away. How many wars had been fought for women of such beauty? How many poets were driven mad trying to find the words? How many painters languished in their attempts to capture it? Omar could do nothing but allow himself to weep freely, moved by her words and beauty.

"It is time we step out of the shadow of the corporate heel that keeps us low. Join me in verse as we honor Lucia's departure and turn towards our captors and voice our grievances."

Slowly the crowd of onlookers turned away from the podium. The funeral program opened back up in Omar's HUD to the selection of the song that they were to sing. A countdown began. A lone flute rose off in the distance. The melody Omar had heard previously that day could be heard. Other mourners began the reverent lyrics to Simon and Garfunkel's "Sound of Silence."

Since the funeral was to be livestreamed and monetized to help cover the cost of the service, international copyright laws forbade them from singing the song in concert. The work-around for this was that the attendants would be broken up into several sections, each section singing at different times. This would jumble the tune enough to escape the automated censors that recorded everything in the mall. Since the practice was commonplace, it wasn't hard to find a program that synced up the singers.

Omar turned his back to the podium and waited his turn. Staring at a wall of dimly lit pods, his timer reached zero, and he began.

"Hello darkness, my old friend…"

Audio implants in Omar's ears isolated his voice. His section was accompanied by a keyboard. He tried to stay in key, but Omar wasn't musically inclined, and at some point, he stopped singing. Switching off the audio filter, he listened to the noise of the other singers that permeated all around him.

Omar closed his eyes and leaned back, allowing waves of vocals to wash over him. He distinctly heard different sections of the congress sing out.

"The words of the prophets…"

"The words of the prophets…"

"The words of the prophets are written on the subway walls."

That resonated with him. It reminded Omar of the dream he had had earlier that day. *Why?* he thought.

Looking around, Omar noticed everyone was standing with a look of resolve. As the beautiful chaos of the song reached a natural crescendo, he turned around to see that Lady Desh, the pallbearers, and Lucia's body were gone. The entire dais was bare except stray flowers left behind.

Panic began to rise in Omar, and he tried to force his way toward the stage. Still, no one budged. They were, for better or worse, locked in where they stood. He sent Lady Desh a text and received the same out of office reply. The song ended, and Grandfather returned to the podium.

"Today is a day of mourning. We shall celebrate Lucia's life with a festival starting tomorrow and continuing into the weekend. Lucia's was a life that deserves to be honored with a feast, as it was her passion to nourish all of us. Thank you all for coming."

"Where'd they go?" Omar turned to Fritz.

"Who?"

Still unable to make his way through, Omar pointed to the now vacant stage.

"Lucia's body. Lady Desh. The men in white. Where'd they go, freak?"

"I don't know, Chief."

Omar's panic rapidly formed into anger. He pushed forward. Chief Hernandez tried calling Lady Desh only to get a similar reply as the text. Nothing. As mourners dispersed, Chief Hernandez realized no one but him had reacted to the disappearance. He saw Grandfather leaving.

"Grandfather! Grandfather, I need to speak with you," he yelled over the crowd. A procession of mourners surrounded the platform, taking turns laying flowers at the now empty stage.

"Over here, Chief," Chief Hernandez heard in his ear. Looking up, he saw Grandfather make eye contact and wave him over to the far side of the stage. Grandfather was being helped down the stairs by several men Chief Hernandez recognized as husbands to Grandfather. Finally catching a break with the crowd, he made it to the elder. Grandfather placed his hand on the small of Omar's back and led him as they walked from the stage.

"Where have you been, Chief? We saved you a place for you at the funeral."

Omar took a hit from his vape. "Yeah. I'm sorry. I tried to get there but the crowd. Do you know where Lady Desh went? Or the body, for that matter?"

"Well, if you had made it on time, you would've known."

"I'm sorry, Grandfather. I'm really trying my best here."

Grandfather Sandoval stopped, smiled, and patted Omar on the cheek while looking into his eyes. "We know, son. We know." Grandfather continued walking. "Now, I need to speak with you privately. There is much you should know about Lucia's work. There is much I need to show you."

Before Omar could answer, his HUD rang. It was Johnny.

"Sorry. One sec, Grandfather. Johnny, where've you been?"

"Hey, Chief. Sorry I've been entertaining Detective Williams. He'd like to see you. Where should I send him?"

"Why didn't he call?"

"I caught him just as we was walking in. Thought it was best to hold him up while the funeral was going on. You make it on time?"

"No. One sec." Omar turned back to Grandfather Sandoval. "I'm sorry, Grandfather. I need to go. It's about Lucia's case."

"I see." Taking a handkerchief, Grandfather gently brushed off some puke from Omar's lapel. Grandfather continued, "Lucia was always worried about others' wellbeing. You should go get a bite to eat, Chief. Why don't you go to Harlen's Pub? I'll let them know you're on your way. It's on me tonight. For Lucia. We'll speak soon."

"Thank you, Grandfather. I'll swing by first thing tomorrow so we can talk. I promise." Chief Hernandez returned to the call, "Johnny? Send him over to Harlen's. I need to eat. Oh, and Johnny, see if you can track down Lady Desh. She had guns on stage during the funeral."

"Holy shit. Are you sure?"

"Yeah. We need to figure out what the hell she was thinking. Oh, and um… look, the Tribunal has decided to throw a festival. Let the guys know we're going to need them to do overtime. Maybe get some more help down here as well."

"No problem, Chief. On it."

Omar started to walk to the north end of Alameda absentmindedly.

"You okay, Chief?"

Omar looked back to see Fritz still standing there. "Yeah, man. Check you later. And the thing about the thing—could you maybe get back to me as soon as possible?"

Fritz pointed to his head. "I'm already on it," he said with a smile.

"Great. Thanks, man."

Omar continued walking down the long stretch of the thoroughfare that made up Alameda. Chief Hernandez's heels clicked against the red brick tile flooring as he weaved past mourners returning to their pods. In the center of the mall, there used to stand benches and greenery shaped like giant eyes looking straight into the ceiling. Long since removed, replaced by pods, the only memory of their existence was the cracked cement poured after the eye-like structures were all torn out. Years later, foot traffic in Alameda seemed to roll along the tiled floor like waves ebbing and flowing against walls. Wherever possible between stores, artistic renderings of what the mall used to look like were painted, now mostly covered by pods, obscuring what was with what is. Various acts of grieving were on display as well. In a sense, now that everyone was a little more spread out from the funeral, it felt like groups of folks weren't trying to out-mourn each other. Bottles of home-brewed and home-distilled drinks were passed around. An old woman placed a bottle in Omar's hands. He took a long pull of the white liquid, allowing it to burn his throat in hopes it would clear his mind. He handed it back.

"*Libertad, jefe.*" The old woman saluted.

"*Libertad, señora?*"

"*Libertad es justo otra palabra para decir 'no quede nada que perder'.*"

"Right. Freedom."

Chief Hernandez made his way up a shallow incline and looked back over his shoulder down the mall.

It had been a strange day. First, the murder of an innocent woman, then that woman's unorthodox funeral. Things just didn't add up. Sure, Omar recognized that he had fucked up getting high in the middle of the day like that. But still, everything seemed to add up to Chief Hernandez missing something. Something important. Alameda ran smoothly. It always had. The Tribunal managed what needed to get done. The chief and his small team acted like armed janitors cleaning up the outside trash that blew into their home. The communities operated as defined. A small village of like-minded folks surrounded by a wilderness made up of a cement desert. People were supposed to feel safe in Alameda

Omar passed the enforcers outside El Corazon. They were all dressed in white as well, just no veil. None of them were off-duty security. Omar could hear a lot of activity going on inside.

"Is Lady Desh in?" Omar asked one of the guards.

"No, Chief. She hasn't returned from the funeral yet. Can I help you?"

"You guys seem busy."

"Getting ready for tomorrow, Chief. Care for some house mix?" The guard offered a bottle to Omar. Omar took a pull from it and handed it back. As the liquor made its way to Omar's stomach, he could feel it protest the drink.

"Freedom, Chief." The guard responded in a toast before taking his own pull from the bottle. Omar nodded and went on his way.

Omar made it to the stairs on the north end that led up to the second floor, right next to Garden Three.

Lying on the east side of the building just north of El Corazon, Garden Three was shut down for the night. The garden only operated when the morning light hit it and closed shortly after noon. More focus was on the late-day gardens that produced more food. Like the other gardens, Garden Three used to be an entrance. The entrances were closed off now to keep outsiders out. One-way emergency exits were installed elsewhere throughout Alameda to replace the closed entrances. You could look into the garden through the clear plastic sheeting that separated it from the rest of the mall. Omar stopped to look at the structure while enjoying a few puffs from his vape. He looked at the densely packed green wall he could barely make out through the dew-covered plastic sheeting. Droplets of moisture collected into large beads that cascaded down the sheet from the upper levels, like raindrops on a car windshield. He got lost in the delicate ballet of rain. Finally, they found their resting place at the receiving reservoir at the base. Sometimes Chief Hernandez heard a mechanical sound, and the wall of green shook and vibrated, causing the water beads to run down the sheet.

Omar had noticed the garden's slow progression in time only passively. He remembered how small and weak everything had looked when he first arrived. Far different from the lush forest that stood before him. He never stopped to appreciate it. It just was. He wondered how much of Alameda had changed without him fully aware as he climbed the stairs to Harlen's Pub.

Omar sat working his way through a wet chimichanga at the bar. Harlen's Pub was dimly lit with LEDs imitating low amber flames in small table lamps. Brown wood paneling covered the walls, giving the place an old New England tavern feel. A light mist of vape circulated the air, helping the customers feel the effects of their drinks. Omar looked up as Jack made his way through the crowded establishment. Jack rolled his shoulders once more to adjust his posture before sitting down to Omar's right. Jack sat turned to face Omar with his right arm leaning on the bar.

"Is Alameda always this packed this late at night? I had a hell of a time walking across it. Probably would have been faster if I got back in my car and drove over."

Omar washed his food down with a beer and wiped his face.

"Mourning. It's probably going to be like this for a while. Where's your partner?"

"Transferred. Didn't like working with me. Said I wasn't involved enough in the job or some shit."

Omar started laughing between bites of food. His cheeks packed like a squirrel, he slapped Williams on his back. "Sounds like a hell of a marriage. Let me buy you a drink to help you celebrate the divorce." He flagged the nearest waitress.

"Yes?"

"I'm done here. Could you please bring us two double bourbons on the rocks? Oh, and please switch it over to my personal tab." Omar turned to Jack. "Just a second, Jack. I need to do something before I forget." Chief Hernandez stared off for a second while he sent Grandfather a thank you text for the meal he had just eaten. Omar turned toward Jack. "Okay,

Jack. So, are all the new detectives like her or did you just get lucky on the draw?"

"Shit, ever since they built that new campus up by Sac, all the new detectives think they've been educated. I say they should have to put time on the streets before they're allowed to climb rank."

"There wouldn't be anybody left who would want to be a dick if that were the case. We were lucky. We started just before the world really went to shit."

"Yeah." Jack leaned in closer to Omar. "I still think about the time with the eggs when we were in academy."

"Oh? I haven't thought much about that in a while."

"First, you get Spacy to let you crack the eggs on his head. What was it for? One hundred credits?"

"Nah. Cheaper. I got him down to fifty. If you can believe that. Yeah, fifty credits if I could break all the eggs on his head."

"And the look on his face when you told him, 'You know? I'd owe you some credits if I break this last egg. I think I'll just hold onto it.' He looked like he was going to stroke out right then and there."

The waitress returned with their orders. Jack caught her before she left. "The next one's on me. Keep them coming."

"Sure." She cleared the remainder of Omar's dinner.

"He had some endurance, too. He chased me all over campus, trying to get at that egg. You know that's why he washed out?"

"'Cause of a couple of eggs?" Jack said.

"Well, a dozen." Omar chuckled. "No, he washed out because everyone called him Eggy instead of Eddy. He couldn't take a joke."

"Well, he was always a stiff shirt. I wonder what happened to him."

Omar looked down at his glass and let out a soft whistle. "He's my boss."

71

Jack laughed. "Of all the rotten luck. Are you kidding me?"

"Nope." Omar raised his glass. "To the Force. They'll never find a better pair of dicks"

Jack raised his glass with his left hand and clinked it against Omar's. "To Tac. I get in trouble if I'm streamed saying it the other way."

"Christ. Well, to Tac, then." Omar drained his glass and placed it so that the waitress could see. "So, what brings Tac's finest to this part of town?" Omar said *Tac* like it left a dirty feeling in his mouth.

Jack reached into his pocket and produced a vape cartridge. It was Omar's brand of wolfberry. Jack slid the cart across the bar.

"Detective De La Torres wanted to run you in for withholding evidence and trafficking a controlled substance."

"Trafficking. Woowee, they do make them bright at that new academy. Still, she is filled with piss and vinegar. I'll give her that much. I thought all resources were pulled. Case closed and all that shit." Omar pocketed the cart.

"Yeah. I had to explain to her it was a whole lot of nothing to stir so much shit up for."

"The academy." Omar tonged at a piece of food stuck in his teeth. "Huh, I guess I'll have to go to State. You know? See if I can't find anything more about Lucia."

"You're not a cop anymore, Omar. You can get in trouble for that."

"I guess you're right. It wouldn't be a very bright idea."

"Speaking of bright, what's with those all-white ghost fuckers?"

Omar shrugged. "Mourning, I guess. That's new to me."

The bartender came around to pour the next round. "They're not just mourning. They are free of the stream."

Omar and Jack looked at each other. Jack laughed. "What?"

"They have figured out a way to remove themselves from

CENCOM collecting all their data. They still live here but apart."

Great. Now I have a fucking offline cult to worry about, Omar thought to himself.

The next round was poured, and Jack raised it up with his left hand in salute. Omar felt his buzz starting up.

"What should we toast to now?"

"To Lucia."

"To Lucia, then." Both men emptied their glasses in a gulp. Jack asked the waitress for another.

"So, what's the deal with this funeral? They always do this when someone dies? The flowers, the banners. Shit, is this all because of those fucking weirdos in white? Seems exhausting."

"Nah. This was—well, shit, Jack. I don't really know what this was. Usually, we—well, if the person was liked, there would be a small service, and the urn would be out for people to pay their respects. Nothing out in the thoroughfare, mind you. Just, you know, usually in their pod or community center. Usually, no one but the next of kin even notices when someone passes. Lucia was different. She was smart, you know."

Omar was enjoying his buzz. He decided to slow down and sip his drink.

"Ah, hell. I was at State just the other day, Omar. That place is filled with smart kids. What made her so fucking special?"

"None of those smart kids came from Alameda. Look around. You see these people? This is it. This is all they will ever know. There is no chance for any of them to know anything different. You can't sell them anything. From where they're at, this is the best they can hope for… until Lucia came around. Lucia had all the potential to leave. She had what they all hoped they could have, and she chose to stick around and help as much she could. There may be thousands of intelligent people over at that university, but in Alameda, they had just one. And that one had them. And now that hope she gave has been snuffed out in front of them. One more loss in a long line of losses. Life is cheap. Hope is mythic rare, if not fucking legendary. These people, these folks—this is it. This is all they will ever get. No matter how hard they work. No matter how hard they try. They will never climb out of this hole. I've been sitting here, marinating. Just watching over the years, I've come to one conclusion. That the system that keeps us alive is also keeping us in place. They signed a contract to live here, sure. All their freedoms signed over to protect corporate liability. This makes sense for CENCOM but leaves them with very little space to maneuver. I don't know a single human being living here that isn't in deep fucking debt. They have nothing to show for their hard work except a mountain of debt. And that debt keeps the slaves in their pen."

"Fucking slaves. Come on, Omar. They signed a contract. They're leeches at best. How many of these 'folks' are actually working?" Jack said.

Chief Hernandez finished his drink and squared up. "I'd watch it with the leeches shit, Jack. We go way back, but I won't tolerate you degrading these folks. As far as work is concerned, many more are trying to work than not. I know. I run collections for CENCOM. It's a stone's throw between them and you."

"All right. Relax. Fuck, when did you get so high and fucking mighty?"

Omar waved for another round. Gripping his glass, he played with the ice. "You know when. I did what I was told. And what did I get for it?"

"Christ, Omar, you shot up a bunch of people during a food riot."

"I was following *orders*."

"That's right! This is why Commander Evens is now Inmate Evens for life, and you are here. Free. Able to come and go as you please. Off the radar. All thanks to CENCOM. So relax."

They sat quietly for a minute. Jack set his hand on Omar's knee.

"Hey, I've missed you. Let me take you back to your place? I'll suck your dick," Jack asked.

Omar slumped down in his chair, sucking the liquor off the ice still in his glass. He pulled away. "You'd better go."

"Right." Jack signaled for one more round and to wrap up his bill. He stood up, rolling his shoulders as the waitress set the last two drinks down.

"Enjoy the last round, Omar." Jack turned for the door before turning back quickly. "Oh, was there ever anything to give Detective De La Torre?"

"Who fucking cares? The Force closed the case."

"Right." Jack turned around and started walking for the exit. He was one table over when Omar stopped him.

Omar let out an exacerbated sigh, "Hey, Jack."

"Yeah?"

"Go downstairs. Head south. About halfway down the mall, you'll find a path that leads to the old movie theater. You'll find what you're looking for there. Just don't tell them you're on the Force."

"Tac, Omar. It's Tac now."

"Same difference."

Omar worked his way through the two drinks alone, then several more, pausing only to chase the amber liquor down with long pulls of his vape. Seating and talking with Jack brought back all the old anger. It was going to be a hard night for Omar. He sat, reminiscing of the last time Jack, and he spoke.

They had just arrived at Omar's studio apartment after a day of internal affairs questions. Jack hadn't spoken to Omar the whole car ride. Bursting right into questioning as soon as they walked through the apartment door.

"This isn't like the other times, Omar. I can't make this just go away. What were you fucking thinking?" Jack asked.

"It was a night operation. Through the goggles, I couldn't make out individual targets. I called—"

"Who do you think you are talking to? That shit is not going to cut it with me. What the actual fuck were you thinking?"

"Jack, can you pretend for just a moment that I'm having the worst day of my life right now? Can you just? For a moment." Omar was tired, and his nerves felt fried. He stood up and made his way over to the cupboard, where he kept a bottle for nights Jack stayed over. Pulled out the bottle of bourbon, two glasses, and the spare vape needed to get drunk. Omar poured two healthy doses of the brown liquor into the short tumblers and handed one to Jack. He took a hit from the vape before handing it over as well. After a long pull of the brown liquor, Omar topped of his drink before sitting in his chair and stared at the floor.

"Fuck, Omar. Take it easy. You don't normally drink."

"Sit down," Omar asked meekly.

Jack sat down on the couch right next to Omar's chair.

"It felt like I was back in Colorado," Omar began. "As soon as I was assigned to riot suppression on the gun ship. You know? It was that old us-versus-them shit. I hated them. Through the goggles, I didn't see individuals. It was just a mass of enemies I needed to eliminate, so that we can go back to the way things were. I want to be a cop again, Jack. So, when the order came in, I didn't even hesitate."

"So, you didn't see those fucking kids?"

"It was midnight in the middle of a fucking riot. What were they even doing out?"

"DID YOU SEE THOSE KIDS?"

"Yes." Omar began to cry.

Jack looked at him for a bit and got up. Finished his drink before heading to the kitchen. Jack stopped halfway and placed his hand on Omar's shoulder. Omar tilted his head and laid it on his hand. To Omar's surprise, Jack jerked his hand away before walking into the kitchen. Rinsed his glass in the sink and placed it in the dishwasher. Jack slowly walked back into the room and picked up his coat.

"Omar, I need you to listen to me. I need you to hear what I'm about to say to you. Understand?"

"Okay," Omar said quietly.

"You are not going to be a cop again. They are never going to allow you to return. You may find yourself lucky to stay out of prison. But I doubt it."

Omar's tears began to fall with such veracity he saw blurred drops cascade into the tumbler.

"I can't go down with you, Omar. This is going to be goodbye."

"No, Jack. Please. I can't. Please, I love you. I can't do this without you."

"I wish I felt the same. But the truth is you were always just a nice distraction. A distraction that has now become a threat to my wellbeing."

"No, Jack, please. I was following orders. You can't leave me for following orders."

"Omar, it's not the orders. You weren't thinking. I'm tired of cleaning up after you."

Omar crossed the room and grabbed Jack's arm, trying to draw him in for a hug.

"Cleaning up after me! It's always been a two-way street, Jack." Omar tried to calm himself. "Don't be this cold. Please. I love you. Please, don't. Not now."

Jack pushed him off and made his way out the door. "It's for the best, Omar," Jack said before closing the door behind him.

Omar's heart was broken.

They hadn't talked since. Even though detective Jack's offer was enticing, Omar still felt deeply for Jack. Too much time had passed.

Back at the bar, the bourbon super stimulant combo was helping Omar block it out. Feeling just right.

When he finished the last one, Omar over-tipped the waitress and picked up a bottle to go. He saw a distressed-looking young woman in a dark corner of the pub. As he got closer on his way out, he noticed the bloodshot look of someone who had been crying staring at him. Chief Hernandez remembered seeing her in El Corazon earlier that day. As Omar passed her, she called out.

"Chief Hernandez?"

"Shit," Omar mumbled to himself and tried to sound soberer than he felt. "Yeah?"

"Can I speak with you? It's about Lucia."

Omar placed his bottle on the table and joined the young woman in the booth. "Okay. Go ahead."

"My name is Gabriela Harrison. My friends call me Gabby. I was one of Lucia's few friends."

"Oh. Sorry for your loss. Um... what can I help you with?"

"Are you going to go to the university?"

"I hadn't planned on it. The way these things go nowadays, I'm expecting to be told to shut this whole thing down after twenty-four hours. Not enough resources, you understand. Unless I have good reason to keep going. Besides, I don't have any authority outside of these walls."

"Could you go and ask just as a concerned citizen?"

"Sure. I mean, I suppose so. But why the university?"

"Lucia said she was doing important research on the Mars problem. I'm not sure what she was doing exactly. She explained the Mars problem was just PR jargon to address Earth's inability to continue to feed its population. She had a major breakthrough with her code that she was excited about. Then a couple of days ago, she got distant. I just have this feeling it's the reason why she's... she's... dead."

"I see. Did you see that man I was with? His name is

Detective Williams. You go talk with him. He'll be able to help you. Not me."

"Lucia was close to Grandfather, so I went to him first. Grandfather said to only trust you about this."

"Grandfather said that, huh?"

"Yeah."

"Hmm. You'd better not be lying. I'm meeting with him tomorrow. He'll tell me if you're lying."

"I'm not."

Omar took a hit from his vape while he studied the young woman. "Okay, okay. I'll think about it. But I'm not promising anything. Understood?" Omar struggled to get out of the booth and picked up his bottle. "Who do you think I should speak with at State? If I decide to check it out."

"Professor Larson. She runs the programmable biology lab that Lucia studied at."

Omar opened a notepad in his HUD. "Larson. Programmable biology. Got it. And this is all on your hunch?"

"Yeah."

"If I find anything, I won't be notifying you. Understand? It goes to the Force. If you hear of anything, it comes to Williams or me. If Grandfather said you can trust me, I'm telling you that you can trust him."

"Yes, sir."

Omar stumbled out of Harlen's Pub, back down the stairs, and called Johnny while he made his way home. The fairway had calmed down, it seemed. A small faction of workers set up white banners with blue roses everywhere. They worked swiftly but quietly to not disturb the residents asleep in their pods.

Pods had been marketed as soundproof. To be more precise, they were space-age sound-reduction technology. Omar never had to stay in one here, but he heard it muffled more than blocked, leaving the occupants to sleep through a sometimes very loud murmur. It was etiquette for those traveling the thoroughfare to speak in hushed tones and walk softly after 9. Patrolling the grounds at night felt more like a headmistress patrolling a school of orphans. And it reminded Omar of barracks living on the Force.

"Hey, Chief."

"Report. How we doing, Johnny?"

"Everything is quiet for now. Most residents are in mourning and keeping to themselves. We have shipments of stuff coming in per Lady Desh. And she is nowhere to be seen."

"For fuck sake."

"Yeah. I went looking for her like you asked. Nothing. Her partner is gone, too. Two men and a woman are overseeing things at El Corazon, Chief. It gets stranger. Lucia's body is missing. We've been contacted by the morgue. Lady Desh borrowed the body for the ceremony. She was supposed to have it back by 9. They're pissed." Omar looked at his HUD to see that it was almost ten.

"Is it too late to shut this festival down?" Omar asked.

"I don't see how we can, Chief. I have three more refrigerated food trucks waiting outside with calls to the office of more on the way. You going to stop our residents from receiving free food?"

"No."

"How much money does Lady Desh have?"

"Well, she was famous. Apparently, a lot more than any of us had guessed. What the hell she was doing here with all those credits is beyond me." Omar stopped walking and hit his vape as he looked around.

"Chief, you there?"

"Yeah, give me a sec." Alameda was visibly in a state of flux. Food could relieve both the stress of an empty stomach and the ever-increasing mountain of debt. On top of that, it eased the sense of loss these folks were feeling. Stopping the festival now would throw this place into a state of chaos.

"Well, it looks like we have no choice but to go with it. Did you request more help from head office?"

"Yeah. CENCOM says they will look into it but would rather we shut the festival down and remember to submit a request for additional labor one month in advance."

"Right, I'll remember to schedule the next murder in advance. Sheesh."

"Chief, I know you are still supposed to be on a break—"

"Yeah, yeah. No worries. I'll be back tomorrow for sure to help out. This is going to be too big to leave you hanging. Johnny, you've been doing a great job. Thanks for all your hard work."

"Thanks, Chief."

"Moving forward, don't waste effort on Lucia's case anymore. I'll handle things from here on. Just focus on the guys and the festival."

"Well, I hate to give you more bad news."

"Oh, shit. What now?"

"No scans. I had CENCOM diagnostic look at the scanning program and the files. The files were corrupted non-repairable, and there is nothing wrong with the scanner. By this point, it is not picking up much of anything."

"Well, maybe I'll get lucky the old-fashioned way?"

"What was that, Chief?"

"Ah, nothing. Keep up the good work."

"Anything else?" Johnny asked.

"No. I'm going to turn in for the night. I'll touch base with you tomorrow."

"Roger that. One more thing, Chief. I don't know if you monitor the news, but there was quite the buzz over Lady Desh revealing herself tonight. That funeral is trending." Johnny blinked out of Omar's view.

"Shit," Omar muttered to no one in particular.

He tried calling Lady Desh himself. Nothing.

[Chief.Sec.O.HERNANDEZ]: @THEGRANDDUCTHESSOF-
DESH You need to call me. Now. Please.

Omar continued back to his apartment. Even with a proper buzz, he had an uneasy feeling growing. He pulled the wrapper off the bottle, unstopped it, and took a swig. He tossed the trash as he passed a receptacle. It should have been a short stroll between Harlen's Pub back up to his apartment at this hour, but the workers that were setting up for the festival crowded the streets. Not wanting to wake anyone up, Chief Hernandez took it easy. Each click of his boot heels sounded like a gunshot in his ears. In actuality, all the pods acted as a natural dampening blanket.

Chief Hernandez opened a maintenance door to cut through the mall using its corridor. There were two sets of maintenance corridors that ran the length of Alameda. Some sections were open for residents to exit through in case there was an emergency. Most of it was only accessible if you had the right keys. The narrow hallways were barely large enough for a single person pushing a dolly. The cleaning bots were the primary residents in the corridors, moving trash and whatnot to and fro. Omar liked to use the corridors to head home late so the residents didn't see him intoxicated. Back on the south side of Alameda, Omar exited and headed for the closest flight of stairs.

Omar saw others like him, junky compatriots beginning their own nightly bottle and vape. Barely lucid with a thin connection to reality. Their eyes twitched and flickered to whatever stream they had passing through their HUD. Settling in for a long night of chasing or hiding from demons. He passed Mrs. Walker's coffee stand locked up for the night. He poked his head over the counter to make sure no one had snuck behind it to steal a free spot to sleep in. All clear.

Omar wished he could relax when he made it back to his place. He felt nervous energy and couldn't figure out why. He looked around and decided to pick up. *Maybe I can tire myself out*, he thought. He went to the bathroom, where he had left his pail. Picked the pail up and made his way to his side table. Carefully placing his new bottle of bourbon down, he picked up the dead soldiers scattered here and there and put them in the pail. Each time he filled his bucket up, he took a swing from his bottle and walked the pail out of his room to a recycling bin. After three trips, all the bottles were dumped. He went to work on his clothes, kicking and pushing discarded articles of clothing into a big pile that he heaped into a sack that he used to drop off his clothes. Looking at himself, he realized he was still in his dress uniform. A large guacamole splotch had made its way onto his shirt, so he stripped down and threw them in, too. Each task completed, he rewarded himself with a hit of the bottle. Still, he didn't feel like he could sleep. *Should I reorganize my closet or clean my gun?* he thought.

It was only halfway through cleaning his service pistol that he remembered he had slept, sort of, at the movie theater. He stopped what he was doing and tracked down where he had placed the nighthowler earlier that day.

Omar sat naked on the edge of his bed, staring down at the cart of nighthowler for a long minute. It was heavy shit, to be sure. He had no idea what was in it. But it did allow him to sleep in the middle of the day. Maybe it would tonight. Omar wanted to stay frosty for tomorrow. Regardless of what may or may not come his way, he had a sense that there was something in the air. It was going to be a big day. Deciding whether he should take a hit and sleep or have a restless night of tossing and turning, he felt the weight of the cart in his hand. He shifted it back and forth between his fingers as he mauled over whether or not he would try it again. He took a swig from his bottle,

"Fuck it." Swapping out the carts, he inhaled the sweet aroma of the nighthowler. Immediately, his eyes got droopy.

Shit. I took too much. Omar began to panic and swapped the carts back out and took a big hit of wolfberry.

"That'ssss betterrrrrr. Hahahahahahahahah."

A metallic echo chamber enveloped his mind. Omar noticed that his room was popping.

"Iiiii diiid aahh grreat joooob cleannnnniinng myyy rrr-rrooommmmmmm. Haaaaaaaa. Mmmmmyyy voicessssss issssss fffffucked. Hahaha"

He stretched out on the bed. *This shit is great,* he thought. He reached into the drawer of his nightstand and pulled out a black sharpie. Omar put a "1" on the cart of nighthowler. He swapped out the cart of wolfberry and wrote a "2" on it. He took a hit from 1, then quickly from 2. The walls of his small room exploded out in infinite directions forming a fractal landscape that resembled a ballroom. Omar stood up and paraded around in his fine tuxedo. The guests had all arrived, and he went around greeting them. Everyone was dressed lovely in their fine attire. He flaunted himself for all the ladies and gentlemen to see. He looked down at his barrel chest. His arms felt strong and sure. He seemed to be both in a state of dress and undress and couldn't decide which he preferred. With a flick of his wrist, he transformed between the two. Omar spun around, dancing from one corner of the ballroom to the other. A servant brought him his bottle on a silver platter. He wrote the number "3" on it before throwing the pen over his shoulder, thanking the server, and taking a long pull of the warm amber that invigorated his body.

"One, two, three, one, two, three, one, two, three," he repeated as he danced across his room, cycling from vape to bottle over and over. The guests of the ballroom surrounded him. Their gowns and jackets dissolved away. Their perfect naked bodies pranced around, teasing him. Gleefully, Omar reached out and fondled their soft breast and firm pricks to his heart's content. Perfect asses bounced and jiggled as they played.

Omar fell onto his bed. When he tried to get up, a force pushed his head back down on the bed. Something soft was crammed into his mouth. An invisible hand pinned his ankles and wrist down onto his mattress. A sharp shooting pinprick of pain screamed across his arm. Omar looked down to see the ballroom melted away to once again expose his sad dim room. His hands clutched open and closed as he jerked his arms, trying to break free.

He couldn't move.

An explosion of agony drove across his gut. All he could see was the ceiling. Then another blue and yellow starburst in his vision as pain erupted from his legs, arms, and stomach. Repeatedly blows came from nowhere and everywhere. Omar let out a muffled cry. He instinctively tried to protect his body. From what he did not know. For what seemed like an eternity, the beating continued. Wildly, Omar looked around and saw nothing but the shimmering outlines of some kind of specters standing over him. Slowly, the ghosts materialized into visions of his victims. Lizard-like expressions of those he had killed in Madera morphed from women, children, and men. The eyes glowed yellow and blinked vertically. He could see gills just below the jawline vibrate with each breath of the monster. Omar felt like he was rapidly sobering up. They were there to punish him for his sins.

"We're going to remove the gag, and you are going to answer some questions. Understand?"

Omar nodded. The gag was removed.

"I'm sorry. I'm sorry. Please, don't kill me. I'm sorry. I didn't want to kill you. I was just following orders. Please, don't kill me."

The gag was crammed back into Omar's mouth as he received another beating.

"You don't fucking speak unless spoken to. Do you understand?" Through tear-blurred eyes, Omar nodded again in agreement at the specter he thought was talking. The gag was removed, and Omar let out a soft but suppressed cry, not wanting to get another beating.

"Good. Now, what did you find in El Corazon?"

"What does that have to do with Madera?"

The gag was crammed back in.

"Nagh, nagh," Omar screamed.

Every muscle in Omar's body clinched in pain as he felt an electrical current course through him. His HUD blinked out of existence. He tried to think about what he had found in Lucia's pod, but the beating and remnants of his high clouded his mind.

"El Corazon, Omar?"

"Some family photos. Not much."

"Bullshit. We know she had something. What did you find?"

"I don't know. I don't know." The gag was placed back in. "Nagh, nagh," he screamed as another shock was administered. The spasming from the electricity compounded Omar's injuries from the beating. Every welt, bruise, and fracture pushed back against the involuntary convulsion of his muscles, tensing. An emergency alarm sounded on his HUD. The nanobots in his body were having difficulties numbing and repairing the damage. For a second, the HUD notified Omar that it would contact emergency services. The system froze before the call went through, and Omar's HUD crashed. Omar no longer had the HUD's safety net for the first time in almost twenty years.

Once more, the gag was removed. Through the drug-fueled haze of the beatings and shocks, Omar remembered.

"Grandfather. I'm supposed to meet Grandfather tomorrow. In the garden. He said it was important." The gag was forced back in.

"Fucking lying. Search every inch of this place. Destroy those vape carts. Maybe if we threaten his dope, he can remember."

"Nagh. Pleath, nagh."

The ghostly lizard man waved his head, and the gag was removed.

"I swear to you. Grandfather. Please, don't. All I know is that I'm supposed to meet Grandfather tomorrow and talk about Lucia."

Another wave of his hand and the gag was put back on.

"Destroy that garbage, anyway. Omar, if you're lying or if you're trying to fuck me, I will end you slowly. I will sober you the fuck up and drag this shit on for days. You need to find whatever it was she had and bring it to us."

"Hogh?" Omar asked.

"We'll know."

Omar looked around as his room was tossed by shimmering outlines folded in and out of reality. His clothes were thrown about, and his vape and carts smashed on the nightstand into a thousand little pieces. Small glass shards filled puddles coated the countertop. Omar was continuously electrocuted while his room was trashed. Once finished, the beating began again. He bit down on the gag as the spirits worked him over.

"Night, night, sweet bitch."

Omar's head erupted into sparks as he felt himself slide down the black hole of unconsciousness.

WEDNESDAY
3:56 a.m.

Omar awakened to a shrieking pain throughout his body. He reached up and pulled his own sock out of his mouth. His belt hung loosely around his neck. Slowly, he tried to get up. Omar grabbed hold of the nightstand next to his bed to stabilize himself, only to quickly pull a bloody palm of glass shards back. The HUD was in a reboot state. Ticking off various systems as they came online. His head throbbed, and the room started spinning. Omar threw up, catching the corner of his bed, not making it to his pail before blacking out again.

"Chief. Chief, wake the fuck up."

Omar walked back from the fog of oblivion. He was on his stomach, looking at a puddle of puke. He brought up diagnostics in his HUD. Nanobots were working to repair damage all over his body. Omar had suffered a concussion. Several ribs were either broken or bruised, and his legs, arms, and groin had sustained a form of bludgeoning damage. The nanobots themselves were operating at a limited capacity due to electrical damage. At some point, they had rebooted.

"Chief. You need to wake up now. Come on, Chief. Grandfather Sandoval is dead. You need to get up."

Omar raised a very shaky hand.

"I'm awake. Just give me a second."

"What the fuck happened to you, Chief?"

"I was attacked." Omar turned his head slightly and felt a mild pain. Johnny and two other patrolmen stood over him.

"Yeah, right." Omar heard one of the patrolmen mutter to the other one. Omar tried to move his head with better success this time.

"I was cleaning up, and some kind of spirits came in and attacked me. I was beaten and shocked." Rising up on an elbow, Omar looked down at his body. He was covered in his own filth. There wasn't a bruise on him.

"Okay. Whatever. Chief, you need to get down to Garden Two. Grandfather was found dead. Looks like he hung himself."

"No. I was. I was attacked." Omar brought up the video feed from the night before in his HUD. Looking to see who his assailants were. Per his request, there was no stream accessible to review.

"No. I was… I was attacked. They… they had faces that changed. They held me down and beat me. They wanted to know what I found. I told them…" Chief Hernandez stopped, remembering what he had said the night before.

"You said Grandfather is dead?"

"YES! Get up. You said you'd help us today. The festival started this morning, and we can't keep Grandfather's death a secret for long."

Omar crawled out of bed and headed for the refresher, stopping halfway to catch his breath.

"Fuck. Let's go. He's not going to be any use to us today," Johnny said as he and the other two patrolmen began to leave. "Clean yourself up, Chief. I'm going to have to report this to head office."

"Johnny, stop."

Johnny turned around and looked at the pile of garbage that was supposed to be his boss.

"What?"

"Don't worry about Grandfather. I'll take care of that. Just focus on the festival. Okay?"

"Fuck you." Johnny turned his back and left.

Omar leaned against the wall halfway in the refresher. He felt a pain in his left hand and looked down. The palm was covered in minor cuts and a strange fluid. He sniffed it and figured it was the wolfberry. He picked the glass out of his hand and licked what he could off of it.

Omar crawled back over to his nightstand, sloshing through last night's dinner. His vape and cartridges were all destroyed. Hands shaking, he needed a fix. He licked the palms of his hands and the nightstand, cutting his tongue on tiny shards of glass. Omar stopped only when he realized it was futile. Wolfberry had to be inhaled. It was the only way the nanobots could receive the hijacked code that got you high.

The previous night replayed in his mind. Omar realized no one was going to believe him. He had lived through it, and he barely believed it himself. He began to cry. He didn't know how long he was on the floor. He just lay down and bawled.

After a while, the deep hurt jogged his memory, and Omar crawled to his closet. He removed a small tile on the floor and pulled out a single-use vaporizer. Through tears and halted breath, he took in the stimulant.

The process felt slow, and Omar wasn't sure he had enough operational nanobots to get off. Chief Hernadez remembered the young woman from the night before with his mind clearing up. He picked himself up and took another hit. On trembling legs, he walked to the refresher. Omar opened a small first aid kit next to his sink and pulled out a small metallic tube about three inches long with a trigger. He placed it against his neck and pulled the trigger. His HUD brought up his account and billed him one thousand credits for the nanobots he injected into himself. For a brief moment, he felt a warm buzz pulse through his neck as the bots dispersed through his bloodstream, getting to work. Reading the instructions on the side of the injector, he counted to thirty in his head.

Now that the nanobots were supposed to be dispersed through his body, Omar took a third hit. This time he felt the familiar rush of the wolfberry doing its job.

Grabbing the counter on shaky legs, Omar stood up. He stepped into his shower to clean himself up, stopping at one point to relieve himself. It looked like blood was finding its way into his piss. Omar went through the cleaning cycle twice, thankful that he had the wall to lean on as the spray did its job. He examined his body. If he was attacked, there should have been bruising. Nanobot medical protocols would have prioritized significant injuries, with bruising being the last thing resolved. The HUD showed the nanobots administering medical help. Still, the order in which they were trying to repair his body was strange. Nanobots were supposed to mend major medical issues to less life-threatening concerns. The order in which Omar's nanobots were operating seemed jumbled. The bots had ensured there was no bruising. Without visual confirmation, no one was ever going to believe him. Omar felt like crying again.

He checked his email. There was a notice from CENCOM. Chief Hernandez was ordered to close the Lucia case. All resources were resolved now that she was laid to rest. Another email said that the stream footage he had requested had been deleted. The last email was a formal complaint from the coroner's office that Lucia's body had gone missing. He emailed Lady Desh, asking her to call or schedule a meeting immediately. Just as he sent it, Omar received notice of new mail. He opened it to find that Johnny had cc'd him on the complaint that Omar was unfit, yadda, yadda.

"Fuck him. Ungrateful piece of shit."

Omar got out of the shower and squared up in front of his mirror. Looking at himself in the mirror, one of his eyes had burst a blood vessel and was bright red. The other was just bloodshot. With quivering hands, he shaved, never letting go of his single-use vape pen.

His jaw was sore from clenching it. Every muscle fought against the simplest of requests. Getting dressed was an exercise of putting clothes on with a minimal amount of exertion.

His sidearm was lying on the small desk, halfway put together. He finished the job and checked it. Picking up the second belt, he wrapped it around his waist, snapping the connections to his primary belt and thigh. Omar holstered the gun, shaking his hips side to side to see if it latched adequately. The gun didn't move.

Good enough, he thought.

He reached back into his closet and pulled out his sun trench coat, hat, and respirator. If he was going outside the mall, he would have to protect himself from the elements. Even if he would drive, in the brief moments walking from his car to a building, the valley sun made it horrible to travel in. The combination of sun and wind could eat at the flesh as efficiently as an out of control bacterial infection. He had to search to find his RFID keys. They were still in his dress pants from the previous night.

The previous night's bottle was tipped over but in good standing. Omar picked it up and drained the last third of it. Chasing it with another long pull of the pin. The pin wasn't as nice as his main vape. He had to really suck hard to pull anything out of it.

Omar opened the door to loud rhythmic music echoing throughout Alameda's hallways. He shut the door and went looking for his sunglasses. He found them in his desk drawer next to his personal AC unit. He put the AC unit on around his neck. The cool gentle breeze that blew up his neck helped sober him up. It seemed to ease the thumping of his head. He cranked it up to the full blast. He put the shades on and walked out of his room.

9:00 a.m.

The thoroughfare of Alameda were comically empty. Omar looked up and down the row of pods next to his door. Music was playing and thumping up and down the way. A constant low yammering could be heard of people talking and having a good time. Lights and white and blue bunting had been and continued to be hung all over. But there were very few residents actively celebrating. He checked his HUD—9:00.

Ms. Walker was standing by her booth. Omar made his way over. The pain from the previous night's beating had him walking funny. His body felt as if there was a consistent but low tremor pulsing up and down his spine.

"You look like a cowboy walking that way. You sleep all right, Chief?"

"Half a cup today, Ms. Walker."

The old woman smiled at him.

"I can offer you a full cup today for that price. Courtesy of Lady Desh."

"Courtesy of Lady Desh. Have you seen or heard where she's at, Ms. Walker?"

"Not today. Why?"

"If you do. Let her know I said hi."

"I will. You want that full cup?"

Omar leaned in. "You wouldn't happen to have anything stronger back there, would you? Say, half a cup of coffee and a little something on top to help?"

"Sure!" Ms. Walker reached behind the counter and pulled out an unlabeled bottle of what looked like whiskey. She set the bottle down clear as day on the counter. "Fifteen?"

"You're not afraid CENCOM will see you?"

"I'm not doing anything wrong, Chief. Who cares what data they collect on me?"

Omar nodded his head in agreement with the logic. "Fifteen."

The chime came and after a moment of Ms. Walker pouring the drink, so did Omar's loaded cup of coffee. From the smell, Omar could guess it was halfway decent whiskey.

"Freedom."

"Thanks. Not very busy for a festival, you think?"

"It's still a workday, Chief. It will be crazy tonight for sure. For now, I suspect everyone still has to be at work."

"Right. Thanks, Ms. Walker."

"Are you going to be okay, Chief?"

Not sure what to say, Omar simply shook his head maybe and bit his lower lip before walking away.

He sipped his coffee while he tried to walk. His legs were stiff. The mix of wolfberry, bourbon, coffee, and the whiskey Ms. Walker put in his drink was starting to help numb the pain.

Omar needed to get more wolfberry if he were to survive the day. He reminded himself that Grandfather took priority. Clutching the single-use vape pen in his left hand, he descended the stairs one step at a time, hand hovering just over the railing should his legs give way. He drank his coffee cocktail fast out of fear of losing a single drop. He pushed himself to hurry to Garden Two, where Grandfather had been reportedly found. Each step shot spikes up his calves into his ribs. Breathing through the sharp pain was brutal. Clenching his teeth, the muscles in his jaw ached. He greeted passersby through gritted teeth. Traffic was light. Those who didn't work, who had started to celebrate the night before, were here and there. They ducked out of sight as soon as they saw Omar. The veiled figures Omar had noticed the night before stood out among the residents. About one and twenty people he passed seemed to don the veil. Other residents were wearing all white.

Outside the gate of Garden Two, the podium and stage were gone. The banners still hung on the walls, now with a single blue rose in the middle of them. Two veiled men dressed in white stood on either side of the entrance.

"What are you two supposed to be?" Omar asked.

"Added security, Chief. Lady Desh felt that you would need last-minute assistance with the festival. We are assigned to guard Lucia's memorial."

"And where is Lady Desh?"

"I do not know, sir."

"Fucking bullshit. Are you two armed?"

"Yes, sir."

"Let me see one."

"Chief?"

"Hand it over. Now."

The guard handed over his sidearm. It was a Colt 6520 10mm pistol. Omar inspected it. The sidearm was in a good standing order, with the safety on but one round in the chamber. Even with hands that shook and a vape pen between his teeth, Chief Hernandez skillfully ejected the round.

"How many of you are armed?" Omar asked before taking a pull from his pen.

"I'm not sure, Chief. More than ten that I know of."

"What kind of training, if any, do you have?"

"There is a prerequisite of a military background for the Alameda Guardians, Chief."

"Alameda Guardians? Shit. Where did you serve?"

"Army Mountaineer during the Border Wars, Chief. I fought in Colorado country."

"And you?"

"Army Ranger, State of Jefferson, sir."

"Let me guess. The veil is so CENCOM can't track who is doing what, right?"

"A simple solution to the complex problem of living here,

Chief."

Omar handed both round and sidearm back to the guard.

"Okay, look. Um… spread the word until I speak with Lady Desh and we get this resolved. None of you are to have one in the chamber. Understand? I'll let my people know. You let your people know, okay? Just know that you guys being armed is not okay. I guess you already know that, seeing as you took the fucking precaution of covering your face. I'll take it up with Desh. For now, it boils down to this. I don't want any accidental shootings today. This is fucked. We're supposed to be having a festival, remember?"

"Yes, sir. Freedom, Chief." The guard gave Omar a salute.

"And send word up the chain of command if you've got one. I need to speak with fucking Lady Desh, now! Sponsor or no Sponsor, she is pushing her luck. If I don't speak to her by the end of the day, I'm evicting her."

Chief Hernandez stormed past the guards. He sent an updated text to Johnny about the guns and got no reply. *Little bitch has his panties in a bunch*, Omar thought.

Omar stepped up and walked through the first of the two gates to enter the garden. Part of the Mars problem was water. Every drop of it had to be accounted for. Low-cost greenhouse gardens like the three in Alameda were perfect locations to work on the Mars problem because the water was just as scarce. Or rather, just as costly.

Two gardeners were sitting down, comforting each other. Omar recognized them to be from Pueblo. Omar went to put a water collection suit on from those that hung along the way near the entrance. Water collection suits were required by all to enter Garden Two. When a person left, the suit would be collected. Any moisture on the suit would be gathered and reintroduced to the environment. Every drop was tracked. Omar reached for the suit when one of the gardeners sitting on a bench in the room looked up at Omar through tears.

"Don't bother, Chief," the gardener said.

"Why's that?"

"It's all… it's all fucked up." He began to sob.

The other gardener put her arm around the distressed gardener.

"You'll understand when you see it," she said while comforting her companion. Quietly, she added, "The garden experiments will need to be started all over again."

"Did you guys find Grandfather?"

"Yes," she said.

"Was he alone?"

"Yes."

"Can I ask why? Grandfather usually has a member of his family with him."

"Grandfather asked to be alone. He wanted to say goodbye to the garden before he left."

"Where was he going?"

"He just said a trip. I didn't think he would kill himself."

"Okay. I'll text you guys if I need anything. You should go and be with your family for now."

Omar waited for the automated system to approve his entering into the facility. A red "WAIT" flashed to a green "WALK" in his HUD after he bypassed lockout protocols for not wearing the water collection suit. He walked through the final door into the garden. Everyone who entered instinctively looked up at the three-story tower of an overgrown garden bed elevator that spanned the breadth of the garden.

Omar took a step back. The sheer volume of the vegetable forest was overwhelming. A jungle of vibrant greens, reds, and yellows greeted Omar's sight. The room was brightly lit with spectral-controlled LED lights that hung everywhere. The beds climbed and descended at angles so that water from an upper bed would rain down on a lower bed but that the light was able to reach every plant. This made a natural path between the rows that allowed the gardeners to easily reach every bed. The floor was a plastic grating that collected loose water.

It had been years since Chief Hernandez stepped foot in any of the gardens, and back then, simple beds lined the floor and grew small, weak-looking crops. Walking through the trellises was like nothing he had ever experienced before. If he didn't know better, Omar would have thought he was no longer in Alameda.

From Chief Hernandez's perspective, he counted six trellises. The mechanical trellises looked to be pieced together with whatever the manufacturers could get their hands on. Frames were multicolored and welded together at different places. Something new and shiny caught Chief Hernandez's eye. Every inch of the room was pieced together from whatever the Alameda residence could find except for several pieces of equipment that looked fresh out of the box. The white and black electronics sat on a table against the wall near trellis two. Labeled bottles of water and vapor samples sat in a box next to the equipment.

The garden was the most beautiful thing he had ever seen in his entire life, and it was only a couple hundred yards feet from his front door.

Chief Hernandez walked past trellis after trellis through the garden until he found Mr. Sandoval.

Grandfather's body hung from the zenith of the beds on Trellis Four. An electrical cord wrapped tightly around his neck. He was not wearing a water suit, and the poor man had relieved himself. Chief Hernandez assumed this is what the gardeners meant. The environment must have been contaminated or something. Chief Hernandez went to work scanning the room. He started at Grandfather's body and worked his way back into a systemic pattern he had learned on the Force. From what he could see, the old man had wrapped the cord around his neck down at the bottom of the trellis and waited for the beds to cycle, carrying him to the top. When Grandfather reached the top, his weight finally overloaded the old motor. Chief Hernandez checked the on-off switch for the beds. No power.

When Chief Hernandez was done cataloging his scans, he brought up the previous night's streams. Sections of the footage were missing. Feeds just stopped and started at what appeared to be random. Chief Hernandez slowly pieced together an idea of Grandfather's movements the night before.

Around midnight Grandfather sent everyone home while working alone in his office. Around 2 a.m., he stopped what he was doing, got up, and walked out of his office towards the small grove of fruit trees that grew at the end of the trellises. What made Garden Two different from all the rest was that three quarters through the garden, the beds and the grated floor stopped. You stepped down onto actual soil. Several trees had been planted and were producing small clusters of citrus fruits. Each tree had a lemon, lime, or orange hybrid.

In the stream Chief Hernandez noticed a fresh sapling mound among the trees with white flowers placed at its foot. Grandfather stopped at the flowers and looked down for a while. Something caught his attention, and Grandfather went back to a small lab. The stream dropped again, and Grandfather's hood was off when it returned. He looked to be upset about something. Argued with himself. For a moment, there was a shimmer in the feed. An outline of a man taller than Grandfather's shadow.

Omar's legs buckled. He crawled to the wall as he tried to catch his breath between sobs. Leaning against the wall, he sobbed, realizing that he had, in fact, sent Grandfather Sandoval to his death. For a moment, when he saw the body hanging there, he had hoped he was wrong and that the old man had, possibly due to some emotional state, killed himself.

Chief Hernandez forced himself to continue to watch the stream. Grandfather's arms shot out from his sides like he was wearing a coat that was too small for him. The old man turned and walked back to the garden beds. The electrical cord floated closely behind him. Chief Hernandez stopped and rewound the footage. On replay, the cord floated into Grandfather's hand, and it looked like a CGI glitch in an old video game for a moment. Chief Hernandez played it back again. This time it was clear that Grandfather was carrying the cord. The video of Grandfather tying the cord around his neck seemed to do the same glitchy movement. Throughout the streams, shimmers of men would fade in and out. Every time Omar felt like he had captured one, when he looked back at it, the shimmer was gone.

"Fuck, they're actively editing the footage."

"Fuck who now?"

"Jack?" Omar croaked out.

Jack came strolling around Trellis Three from the front entrance.

"Hey, hey, Omar. Why are you on the floor?" Jack squatted down in front of Omar.

"You got here quick. I didn't know that Johnny called it in already," Omar said trying not to cry.

"I never left last night, remember? The movie theater. Are you okay? What's going on?"

Not sure what to say about his new discovery, Omar just said, "Ah, looks like suicide."

"Okay, I would think you would get those a lot around here. Did you know him?"

"Yeah. You could say that." Omar's hands started to shake, and he hit his vape. He looked down at Jack's shoes, which were covered in a layer of dirt. Omar decided he couldn't do this on his own.

"Jack… Jack, I need your help, man. You know, for old time's sake."

Jack crossed to sit right next to Omar and placed his arms around Omar's shoulders.

"What's going on, Omar?"

Omar could feel his whole body begin to quake.

"Look. Lucia was working on something important. She ended up dead with no footage of her attack. Last night Lucia's Sponsor went missing. The next day Lucia's mentor in the gardens kills himself."

"Well, the loss of a loved one can be traumatizing to the elderly. Didn't I hear that if it wasn't for Lucia, Grandfather's gardens wouldn't even be? That she brought them back from the dead. It could all have been too much for him."

"Jack, I was supposed to meet with him today. He wanted to discuss Lucia with me. And then last night…" Omar trailed off, not wanting to put words to what had happened.

"Last night what?" Jack asked.

Omar forced himself to continue on. "Last night, people who looked like ghosts or outlines came to my apartment, beat me, and asked me questions about Lucia. Jack, I told it—or them—I was going to speak with Grandfather today, and now I think I got him killed, Jack. I was watching the stream, and it looks like someone is actively changing it in real time."

Jack pulled Omar in. Omar felt safe once again in Jack's arms and allowed himself to let go. Between sobs he could smell the old familiar, spicy scent of Jack's cologne and felt like now it could be okay.

"Oh, Omar. It's going to be okay. I want you to listen to what you are saying. Ghosts. Someone is changing the stream. That's impossible. The stream is encoded, not to be fucked with. It's practically carved in stone, man. Look." Omar's HUD chimed a couple of credits in his account. "Go get yourself a drink and pull yourself together. It's on me. It's obvious to me this is getting personal for you. That's not good, man. You need to stay focused. Once you have your head on straight, you'll see this through clearer eyes. Okay?"

"I know that the Force has closed Lucia's case. But for me, could you keep looking into it? You owe me nothing. I know that, but I don't know what's going on, Jack. I just… I just…"

Reluctantly Jack agreed. "Sure. I'll see what I can do. But do yourself a favor, Omar."

"Yeah?"

"Don't tell anyone else about these ghosts."

Defeatedly, Omar agreed. "Yeah."

"Now, did you get a scan?"

"Yup."

"Okay, good. Send it to me, and I'll take a look at everything. Why don't you go Harlan's? Get yourself together. I'll take care of the coroner." Jack helped Omar to his feet giving Omar one final squeeze before gently leading him to the door.

"Thanks, Jack."

"One last thing. Did you find anything else around here you think I should look at?"

"No. Not really, just what looks like samples on a table over there. I hadn't got to the lab yet."

"Okay. Well, I'll take care of it. Go ahead and go. I got this."

"Thanks."

Before walking out of the garden Omar stopped and collected himself. He hit his spare vape pen. Half a dose and it was done. In a daze, he started over to the movie theater.

The more he walked, the worse he felt. He floated in a daze. People passed him only in his peripheral vision. Every once in a while, Omar would check his HUD. The nanobots were working overtime. His legs were at the bottom of the list of things to repair. He went back and checked the list from the beginning. Concussion, broken collar bone, several broken ribs, bruised and fractured legs. Omar got an idea and sent the list to Johnny with a note.

[Chief.Sec.O.HERNANDEZ]: Believe me now?

[Sec.Off.J.WRIGHT]: Are you serious? Lady Desh has armed guards roaming the streets. We're trying to disarm them now. And you are still going on about your self-harm bullshit.

[Chief.Sec.O.HERNANDEZ]: I know about the guns. Check your messages. Just ask to check their firearm and make sure there is no round in the chamber. I'll handle the rest.

[Sec.Off.J.WRIGHT]: Negative. Sent a report up the chain. We're getting back up, and these "guards" are to hand over their firearms or risk being expelled from Alameda.

Chief Hernandez called Johnny. It rang longer than it should have before Johnny answered.

"What do you want?"

"You have no authority to go over my head! You are not to engage with those guards until I have a chance to smooth things out."

"No authority?! You've been out of commission in one way or another for weeks now. I've had the authority. Just because you finally woke up and want to play cop doesn't mean shit. I was going to tell you in person, but fuck it. New orders came in. You are to step down at the end of the week. I will be taking over as Chief of Security. So, if you could do me one last favor before you fade off into obscurity, wrap up the report on Grandfather's suicide. Then you can go climb into whatever fucking bottle or cart you desire. Security Chief Wright out."

He hung up.

Omar stood in the middle of the thoroughfare, staring down at the broken tile at his feet. It was all undone now. Passersby seemed to not even notice him standing there. The weight of his failures began to build on his shoulders. He cycled through them over and over in his mind. Lucia's case was ordered to be closed. Grandfather would be considered a suicide, and Jack took over that. Fucking Lady Desh was building some kind of religious cult. That ungrateful piece of shit Johnny turned on him.

Omar realized that at that moment, Johnny had been playing him the whole time. To what end?

Probably positioning himself for my spot, he thought.

He felt like crying again, but he had just enough resolve inside him to keep him from doing it. Maybe he just had had enough. Mindlessly, Omar put one foot in front of the other. He didn't know what he would do without his job. He went to take a hit from the backup vape. Nothing. He looked up and realized he was standing in front of the double doors that led to the hallway of the movie theater.

Fuck it, he thought to himself. *I might as well go get high.*

Omar stomped off down the corridor to the movie theater. He passed several more Alameda Guardians. The guards gave Omar a salute.

"Freedom."

"Yeah, yeah. Freedom," Omar replied haphazardly.

Nothing seemed to matter anymore. *What were they going to do, fire him?* That had already happened. He checked out his bank account. He thought he had enough credits to climb into the movie theater and burn himself out over the next month. And when he was down to his last couple of credits, he'd get himself a bot killer and take care of it all. Suicide programs were easy to come by in Alameda. CENCOM didn't care if anyone smoked themselves to death. Just so long as they were paid up on their rentals.

Ding.

Omar's HUD chimed, and he looked up to see that he had mail. It was an email from the coroner regarding Lucia's missing body. Apparently, they were pissed it hadn't been returned. He deleted the email.

Not my fucking problem.

Omar passed the tag that read "Freedoms just another word for nothing left to lose." Omar smiled. "You've got that right, motherfuckers," he shouted.

Omar was practically skipping by the time he was inside the lobby. His legs still throbbed, but they no longer screamed with each step. The idea of just saying fuck it all and getting as high as possible was elating. Bathed in the red and purple neon light, Omar smiled. *Yeah. It's not my problem anymore*, he thought.

Behind the counter, the Usher stood fiddling with something. He looked up and smiled. "Chief, what do I owe the pleasure?"

"I've lost everything, Usher. My carts, my vape. I just drained my emergency. I need it all, my man."

"No shit. Here's some wolfberry. I'll get a package together." Usher went to work grabbing boxes from under the counter, opening them up, and pulling a new vaporizer.

"Jesus, Chief. What happened?"

Omar took a long hit. "Ah, that's better. You wouldn't believe me if I told you."

"You'd be surprised. I hear all kinds of interesting stuff."

"Well, you know what? Fuck it, man. Okay. Last night I was partying in my room."

"I like where this is going. Go on."

"So, I'm chasing nighthowler with wolfberry and a bottle of bourbon."

"Fuck, Chief. You should be careful. Mixing code like that could fry you."

"Well, it didn't. It was actually a pretty good trip until…."

"Until what?"

"Until these specters came into my room. Beat me, asked a bunch of questions, and finally smashed all my shit."

"It was probably Tac. Fucking savages."

"Tac? What do you mean?"

"They can do that now. They send out some kind of scentless gas code that allows them to just disappear, just like our vape, man. The code tells the nanobots to just erase them from our view. I bet they can even hack the hacked nanobots to sober you up. Where did I put that charger…?" Usher ducked down under the counter, digging in the back, looking for the charger. "Shame about your shit, Chief. Were they looking for the dongle?"

"What?"

Usher popped back up with the last of the boxes and started opening and putting the equipment together for Omar.

"The dongle. You know, if I knew when I fished it out of your shit yesterday, I would never have given it back to you. CENCOM offered me a pretty penny for it. Do you still have it?" Usher asked with a smile.

Chief Hernandez stared at Usher.

"Did you talk with them? What do you know about the dongle?" Omar asked, confused.

"Well, yeah. They saw in the stream that I pulled the dongle out. CENCOM asked that if it ended back in my possession to let them know."

"Who's this?"

"My CENCOM handler. You don't think I could operate this theater without CENCOM's approval? I have an automated handler. It asks for updates from time to time. Along with their cut, of course."

"Do you tell them about me?"

"Of course, Chief. It's always asking about you. The handler ensures that your supply is quality. CENCOM has a vested interest in ensuring that you're okay. The handler always makes sure you have the best. That is why I was able to offer you the nighthowler. It suggested it. Said you needed to relax. AIs, am I right? Always look out for our best interests. All right, here you go. You're all set."

Chief Hernandez stared in disbelief at Usher. "You work for CENCOM?"

"We all work for CENCOM, Chief. We live in their house and sell what they let us sell. We can only do what they allow us to do, Chief."

Omar thought back to the previous night's beating. It had to have been on CENCOM's orders. Omar realized he was being played but for what end.

"Usher, what's on the dongle?"

"What? I don't know."

Furious Chief Hernandez lost control and reached over the counter, grabbing Usher by the collar. He pulled his gun and crammed it into Usher's face. Remembering how he found Grandfather dead body hanging in the garden.

"What is on the fucking dongle? What did they say?"

"Fuck, man, nothing. Just if I saw it again, I should grab it for them. I swear, Chief. Shit, it's all above board, man. My rent's paid up. I swear."

Slowly Omar holstered his gun and let go of the collar.

"Above board? Fuck you. You fucking snitch." Omar grabbed the carts and new vape and pocketed them. The automation chimed the transaction in his HUD. Of course, CENCOM knew. Chief Hernandez realized just how stupid he had been.

"Not cool, Chief. Don't come back here looking for anything else. I'm done with you."

"Usher, you're done with me when I say you're done with me. If I find out you know more than what you just told me, I'm going kill you."

"Fuck you."

"Yeah, fuck me."

Chief Hernandez stormed out. He sprinted down the corridor, texting Fritz as he ran to the re-pub. If CENCOM tracked the dongle to the Usher, then it may have tracked it down to Fritz.

[Chief.Sec.O.HERNANDEZ]: Hey! @FreakyFritzFreeloader. You okay?

[FreakyFritzFreeloader]: What's up?

[Chief.Sec.O.HERNANDEZ]: I'm heading over. We need to speak in person. Do you know some place private we can talk?

[FreakyFritzFreeloader]: Haha. Just kidding. This is Fritz's out of office bot. Please, leave a message, and I'll get back to you. NAME RECOGNITION CHIEF HERNANDEZ ADDIDUM INITIATED Omar, I'm working offsite and will hit you up when I get back.

Chief Hernandez stopped in his tracks. *Well, at least Fritz was kind enough to use a freaking bot. Fucking Lady Desh, what was she up to?* He hit his vape and thought for a while. It made perfect sense that Fritz had bounced after asking him to look at the dongle. Omar realized he had asked him to go off the grid. *Okay,* he thought, *Fritz is smart enough to go take care of himself. I need to keep working on my end. What do I know?*

The fairway was warming up. Omar went to take off his jacket and realized why he had grabbed it in the first place. He headed to the parking garage.

The growing rage from being played by a fucking bot, mixed with a proper dose of wolfberry propelled him forward. Cutting through one of the re-pubs, Omar used his RFID keys to gain access through the back maintenance corridors. Traveling through the halls saved Omar the hassle of leaving Alameda and walking to the parking garage.

He chipped his way through the door leading to the garage. The garage was an afterthought from Alameda's design. It took up the distance from the face of the mall to Blackstone Avenue. At the bottom of the garage were three stalls for CENCOM Security corporate vehicles. Only one stall was occupied.

Omar walked up to stall number one and pulled the retractable covering off the car. The canvas cover zipped into its storage box, leaving a cloud of dust and soot in the air. None of the guards had much use for the vehicle. Most of his team didn't even know they had it. The door unlocked as Omar reached for the handle.

"Good afternoon, Security Chief Hernandez. Where to today?"

"Programmable Bio Department at State."

"On our way. Please, buckle your seat belt."

Omar sat back in his chair and took a hit from the vape.

"You should know CENCOM has taken a strong stance against drug use. As a company vehicle, drug use while operating the vehicle is strictly forbidden. As such, this is a non-vaping vehicle. You should be more concerned about your health, Security Chief Hernandez. I have taken the liberty to inform your supervisor. Should this behavior continue, you will need to seek medical help."

"Settings. Disable video feed. Disable feed on all calls. Disable health—ah, shit, can you just take the settings from my home operating system and apply them to the vehicle?"

"Completed. Would you like to watch a live CENCOM stream on your trip? I can provide news, entertainment, and sports. Today's top ten streams are—"

"No. Just some quiet, please." Chief Hernandez stared out the window as the car pulled onto Blackstone Avenue in front of a behemoth electric bus and made its way north. All the vehicles were neatly lined up in computer-perfect synchronicity.

Blackstone Avenue was once a main commercial artery through the city. The old repair shops for tires, smog, auto repair, and even stereo installation were obsolete. As far as Omar could remember, no one owned their vehicles. Everyone rented, leaving repairs to the rental agencies whose corporate overlords ensured all modifications were through proper warrantied channels. The selections were limited, based on what the metadata said people wanted. Swipe right for red, left for blue. In reality, anything you could get your hands on, even some items virtually, was wrapped in legalese warranties no one ever read. A person had to be careful not to mishandle said items and void the warranty. The American tinkerer had died along with personal property.

When he was younger, maybe seven, Omar's father took him to a car show. He remembered holding his father's hand while enjoying an ice cream. The showroom he remembered was a simple hanger with sheet metal walls that radiated heat. Fans were everywhere, blowing a hot, dry wind that didn't really help much. The bright lights hung over his head added to Omar's misery, but boy, did those cars shine. Omar's father would excitedly pull him from one car to another as if he were the little boy and Omar, the unenthusiastic parent dragging behind.

"Look, *mijo*. Look how beautiful they are."

He was right. The candy-colored coating of the cars mixed with the brilliance of chrome made each one look like a fine jewel. The lights bounced off polished metal surfaces like stars in the night sky. Some paint jobs were so rich you could get lost in their depth. Omar looked from the cars to his father, who was smiling from ear to ear.

"Look, *mijo*. Do you see? This is what hard work and time can create. We all have such beauty inside us. Never forget."

Omar shook the memory away. What did he know about beauty? Omar's father worked hard at a manufacturing plant. Until one day, a reckless automated forklift crushed him, pinning Omar's father between two pallets. The day at the car show was one of the only times Omar could remember his father smiling.

The streets were covered in debris. The city had long ago given up on picking up this stretch of town. The pod-less would pick through it in hopes of finding anything of value.

The shops along the avenue were a mix of small, filthy, outdated pods packed into either old garages or closed furniture showrooms, repurposed like Alameda to house as many as possible. He clicked the browser icon in his HUD. *What is the current population of Fresno City?* he thought.

The response was quick. "2.5 MILLION RESIDENTS CURRENTLY RESIDE IN FRESNO CITY PROPER."

How many Fresno residents are employed?

"THE BUREAU OF LABOR REPORTS THERE ARE CURRENTLY 581 THOUSAND CITIZENS EMPLOYED IN THE CITY OF FRESNO."

"Huh, a city of the lost," he mused.

Many of the garages had bright red LED lights to indicate that you could share a pod with a body artist for a price. The wares for these spaces walked the street only as far as the garage's parking spaces allowed. Back and forth. Faces covered by beat-up and run-down respirators to help survive the dusty valley air. Some used a simple paper mask that was no use at all. The women's and men's skin had turned to dark leather, cooked in the valley sun. The price of shaking one's ass all day in the heat wearing nothing but a scarf. There was always someone out and about who had scraped enough together for five to ten minutes of enjoyment.

I wonder if they're counted as employed in the Bureau of Labor's report, he thought.

Occasionally Chief Hernandez would spot a mom-and-pop kitchen. All the small-time restaurants looked to have seen better days. Paupers compared to the corporate fast-food buildings that stood on every corner. The foreboding corporate monolith overlooking and beholding all that passes by with its open doors like cathedrals of old.

Come. Break bread at our table. Rest for a moment, but only if you can pay the fee.

The chime went off several times in his ear, and Omar looked up to see the phone icon in his HUD. It was his boss, Commander Spacey. He sent it to voicemail and continued to look out in the world. The chime went off once more.

"Where the hell do you think you're going?" Commander Spacey was annoyed.

"That's a neat trick. I didn't even pick up. I'm going to run a personal errand. I'll be back to Alameda shortly."

"For fuck's sake. There is a full-on riot about to pop off in Alameda, and you're running errands. Get back to Alameda."

"After. There's not going to be a riot. Officer Wright is overreacting. It's just a bunch of residents throwing a party."

"I'm afraid your assessment of the situation is wrong. You need to get back to Alameda. That's an order."

"What are you going to do, fire me?"

"Oh, I see. You think there will be no consequences for your actions. Well, smart ass, there are. For starters, that's a company car. I don't give a shit about whatever it is you think you are doing, and it's obvious you're done with me. So, I'm turning the car around. If you come back with the car, I'll let you finish the week with dignity."

The car turned on its blinker as it made its way over to the median for a U-turn.

"Car, pull up curbside. I'm getting out."

"I am obligated to warn you that the outside temperature is currently over one hundred and twenty degrees with a grading of extremely unhealthy air. Do you wish to continue?" the car retorted.

"Pull the car over. I'm getting out."

Dutifully, after the U-turn, the car obeyed. Omar slid over to the passenger side to get out. He reached for the handle just as the door locked.

"Omar, think about what you are doing," Commander Spacey said slowly. "You can still turn this around for yourself. Even go back to the way things were perhaps. But if you exit that vehicle, you're dead to us. Do you understand?"

Chief Hernandez focused on Commander Spacey in his HUD before replying.

"Yeah? Get bent, Eggy." He covered his face with his respirator, unlocked the door, and exited the vehicle with a little more force than he should have. The door opened, bounced back, and crashed into his arm, forcing him to shove the door open again.

As soon as he had closed the door behind him, the car took off back to Alameda. Omar flipped it the bird. If they were still watching, great. If not, who cares? The gesture felt good.

For a minute, he fumbled, adjusting the respirator, unfamiliar with the device. He couldn't remember the last time he had left Alameda. He fixed his coat, the individual AC unit that hung around his neck, put on his shades, and shored up his wide-brimmed, tan hat. Omar looked at the heat waves rising from the sidewalk in front of him. He tried to rent a ride, but his browser kept timing out. He inhaled deeply and let out a long sigh.

What the hell am I doing? he thought. He grabbed his inhaler, removed the respirator he had just spent so much time adjusting, and took a long hit.

10:45 a.m.

Omar felt manic. Why was this so important to him? What was so important? He began to walk down the sidewalk towards Shaw Avenue. Shaw was the other surface street artery across town. Shaw was to law firms and medical offices as Blackstone was to automotive shops. The once thriving avenue was now almost entirely single-family rental properties from old, converted offices. The intensity of the heat weighed on him, compounding the soreness from the previous night's beating. Immediately, he started to sweat. With nowhere to escape from the sun now, former Chief Hernandez drew inward.

He questioned his own sanity, pushing so hard. Putting himself into this situation after he had a clear green light to climb snuggly into a bottle. Nothing seemed to be what it once was. He was leaning into it. Allowing it all to unravel around him. But why? Lucia was just another dead woman in a long line of dead women he had come across. Two days ago, he had everything he needed. Now he was walking in Fresno in the middle of summer. Walking! His eyes never left his feet. Only looking up at intersections when he would approach the rubberized yellow ramps to cross. Every step was a struggle, and every step a conscious decision to push forward.

Omar's HUD chimed. "Automatic system update initiated. CENCOM personal AC offline while rebooting."

The AC unit around his neck cycled off. The plastic casing started to heat up from the sun and rubbed against his collared shirt.

Heading north, Omar saw a giant holograph being projected into the sky at the intersection of Shaw and Blackstone. The sign was a running set of commercials, primarily for online shops peddling this season's clothes for rent. Omar waited to cross the street. Leaning against the streetlamp, he watched the ads while he waited. One of the ads was for luxury apartments for rent at the River Bluffs complex north of town. The ad promoted a two hundred square foot apartment with holoprojection walls that allowed the resident to live anywhere and anytime. After the virtual tour, the feed cut to a beautiful, happy, neutral couple playing with a dog on green grass overlooking a crystal blue river that passed alongside a lush forest. Free access to Woodward Park for all renters was emblazoned beneath the couple.

Not in this fucking heat, Chief Hernandez thought. It occurred to him that some ad-jockey in Europe probably came up with the idea. More than likely, they had never been to Fresno. Probably never would.

Omar's HUD chimed. He didn't recognize the caller.

"Hello?"

"Hello, this is a pre-recorded message for River Bluffs Luxury Rentals. We noticed you enjoyed our ad. Would—"

Omar hung up the phone and jammed the button to the crosswalk.

"Walk, walk, walk" rang out, and Omar crossed the street, head down, back in thought. He passed a pod-less hiding from the sun under a tree with her dog. When the pod-less woman saw Chief Hernandez, she quickly grabbed her dog and covered it with a blanket.

"No. Please, don't. Not my Spike. He is all I have. I beg you, don't take my baby."

"I'm not on the Force. I'm not here to ticket you for the dog, lady."

"Why else you down here with the rest of us, Officer?"

"Just passing through." Omar continued on.

"He's going to take my baby! Please, someone, don't let him take my baby!"

Omar could still hear her wails well down the street.

The state had outlawed the pod-less from owning pets, stating such ownership was cruelty to animals. Every so often, the Force would come through and confiscate the animals and hand out citations the pod-less couldn't afford. The pets would be humanely destroyed at the pod-less's expense. Often the pod-less would find a new stray cat or dog to have for as long as they were allowed. The streets were always full of all kinds of strays. An endless cycle of loss.

Omar's mind drifted as he walked. He remembered a time when he was six or seven. His school had a Halloween festival that his parents took him to one autumn. The carnival had rides and booths that sold homemade goods. All of it was a fundraiser. Inside the school's cafeteria, someone had erected a small, haunted house out of large, thick gym mats that were stacked like a house of cards. It wasn't very big. It was intended for the smallest of children. Omar spent his last ticket to go in.

He remembered it was dark. The musky smell of old sweat filled the small hallways. Beams of light streamed in through cracks here and there at the joints where mats met. Omar was delighted in the game he and his peers played, jumping out from the corners, screaming, and laughing.

Then the mats came down. Omar never knew what had happened, just that he was pinned between what had been a moment ago a wall and ceiling. Everything went dark, and he couldn't see. He couldn't breathe as the air was forced out of him do to some rhythmic pressure being applied to his back. His joy turned to terror as he realized he couldn't move. The weight of the mats and whoever was on top pinned him to the ground. Omar had all the air knocked out of him, and he couldn't breathe, let alone call for help. Silently, he cried.

Someone grabbed his hand and pulled. Kicking his legs, Omar assisted, fighting to get out. When his eyes adjusted to the light, he saw his mother, who picked him up and held him in her arms. Omar remembered the feeling of burying himself in her shoulder and breathing in the familiar, soft floral scent that calmed all fears.

"It's okay, *mijo*. It will pass. Calm yourself. Don't show your friends your tears. Be brave, *mijo*."

Crossing the bridge over the freeway woke him from his dream. One foot in front of the other. All around him, he was surrounded by the soft swoosh of cars. Omar looked out over the side at the grid of vehicles. Coveting ease and comfort. He was struggling to carry the load of the sun. Looking ahead, he spotted a Chinese recruitment building.

Almost a decade earlier, the People's Republic of China had figured out trans-galactic travel. Immediately, they put up recruitment centers around the world seeking colonists who wanted to get off this planet. A holographic promotion streamed across Omar's augmented reality. "Come inside and enjoy a drink of water as we discuss the future of humanity," it read.

Omar made his way in. Even for a short reprieve from the high temperature, it was worth it. As soon as he cleared the threshold, he pulled his respirator off and breathed in the sweet scent of fresh air. Sweat poured out of the respirator, pooling on the carpeted floor. A man with teeth so white they looked like chiclets and a suit so clean and new it hung as if it was always meant to be there came walking up with a purpose.

"No. You need to leave. Right now, please."

"I just need to catch my breath. Why don't you tell me about what you are recruiting for while I wait?"

"There is nothing to discuss with you, sir. You obviously don't have what we are looking for."

"Oh, yeah? What's that?"

"We recruit families, not individuals. We are not running a charity here. The Promenade is across the street. You can rest there. Please, leave before I have to call Tac."

"Can I get water at least? We did discus my lack of future."

Frustrated at the logic, the clean man walked over to the fridge. But instead of pulling a bag of chilled water out, he reached down and pulled one out of the box next to the fridge. A bag of two hundred milliliters of room-temperature water was tossed at Omar. He fumbled and failed to catch it, then bent over to pick it up off the floor.

"Now leave," the man demanded.

Omar turned around and walked out. Tearing a small hole in the bag, he drank the water greedily, throwing the empty bag at the foot of the door.

The short reprieve now over, Chief Hernandez looked down the road. He wasn't sure if he could make it to State. Omar checked the AC update in his HUD. The HUD indicated that the upload was stuck at two percent. Reluctantly he reattached his respirator and leaned into the march towards the Promenade.

The Promenade was like Alameda. It, too, was once a mall that had been repurposed to be a living facility operated by CENCOM. Omar made his way across the street and double-timed it to the closest entrance. The former parking lot was packed with prefab bungalows filled with the overspill of pods. Doors to the bungalows were propped open with small fans. Fans seemed to hang out every door and window. Slowly turning blades trying to circulate air. Just enough to feel a breeze but not enough to make a difference. The faster the fans spun, the more the occupants would be charged. Electricity was a luxury. Omar looked through a door as he passed. The dark portal housed someone moving about, but he couldn't make anything out. He imagined some miserable person sticky with sweat lying about, not wanting to breathe from the strain. Every window had some kind of reflective material covering it, a hodgepodge mix of aluminum foil and any scrap piece with a reflective side.

The Fresno dust had covered and muted everything with a thin layer of grayish brown.

Omar made it to a set of double doors that opened into one of the Promenade's community centers. A community guard stood just inside the door and stopped him.

"Can I help you with something?"

Not wanting to draw attention, he flexed his old credentials. "I'm Chief Hernandez of Alameda. I'm just passing through. May I come in?"

"Why are you walking?"

"Car problems. I need to get to State, so I decided to hoof it."

"Well, that was stupid."

"You're telling me. Can I come in?"

"Sure. Let me escort you to the other side of the community. I'll alert Promenade's security that you are here."

"That's really not necessary. I'm just passing through."

"Suit yourself."

After signaling for a replacement, the guard led Chief Hernandez through the tight-knit pods. Like Alameda, in this community, the families pulled pods together to create larger living spaces. Modifications were everywhere. Young kids were lying about, eyes closed, hopefully participating in school, more likely enjoying an online game.

Once through, the guard left Omar. Omar was shocked to see how crowded it was compared to Alameda. He had assumed all of CENCOM's housing facilities were the same. However, the Promenade was unbelievably packed, far tighter than Alameda. The Promenade was newer than Alameda, but it was not as well laid out. Alameda had two stories, increasing the walkways both directions and taking advantage of the vertical space. There was a lot of real estate above that was not utilized in the Promenade. Vaulted ceilings are what they used to call them in houses. All that open, unused space was disorienting to Omar. The storefronts that once sold endless, useless goods were smaller than Alameda's and more were residential instead of re-pubs. More people, less workspace.

He checked to ensure that his pockets were secured and his gun latched. Chief Hernandez was confident with this volume of people crammed together, a good number of pickpockets roamed the grounds. He may have been a chief in Alameda, but that didn't mean dick anywhere else.

Halfway through, Omar found a food court and stopped to eat. He was exhausted. While sitting for his number to be called, he checked out nanobot diagnostics for his body. The nanobot repairs to his body from the previous night's assault were all most complete. Now his body was taking a heavy toll just walking down the street. He opened the messages he had been ignoring while suffering through the long walk. A flood of emails came in from CENCOM. Reports upon reports he had to complete after quitting. Exit interview questionnaire, formal resignation doc, relinquishing of CENCOM property, nondisclosure agreements, on and on. He searched for anything from Lady Desh, Fritz, or Jack. Nothing.

The number 1013 dinged in his HUD.

Omar walked over to pick up his meal and was stopped by the server.

"I'm sorry, sir. There seems to be a problem with your account. I can't sell you any food."

"What do you mean? I already ordered it."

"Your account flagged while we were making it, and it says you are unable to pay for this food and I am unable to give it to you. I am sorry for your inconvenience."

"I've got this, Sally." A Promenade Security guard walked over.

"Yes, Officer." Omar noticed the server avert her eyes to the floor as the security officer got closer.

"Thanks." Omar looked at the officer, who gestured for him to sit at a nearby table.

The security officer placed Omar's tray in front of him before taking a chair across.

"We have a considerable amount of lag in this food court. The servers deal with it by making the food before the auto-registers process the bill. Everyone in the Promenade knows to have their ducks in a row before ordering. That way, the servers don't waste food. As I am sure is the case in Alameda, they get billed for waste. Now, you want to tell me why you didn't report to us when you entered our facility?"

Chief Hernandez took a bite of his burger and washed it down with the water he ordered. He took another bite. Through squirrel cheeks, he answered the officer.

"I'm not on duty. I'm just passing through on an errand. Came in to beat the heat."

"Why aren't you driving?"

"We all could use a little exercise, yes?" He chuckled. "Nah, car broke down,. Couldn't get another ride. I decided to walk."

"This errand wouldn't have anything to do with the veiled wackadoos dressed in white, would it?"

A look of surprise crossed over Omar's face, "Veiled wackadoos, huh? No, sorry to say I'm on my way to State for a different matter. When did these guys show up?"

"Yesterday."

"They say what they are about?"

"All we can get out of them is that they are assisting us for some upcoming festival. Call themselves Promenade Guardians."

"Well, we got them over at Alameda. I think it's some kind of new religious bullshit. Have you searched them yet?"

"Should we?"

"Ours are armed."

"Thanks for the intel. I'll pass it along. I must insist on escorting you to the exit when you finish eating."

"Sure. Can I get more water on my way out?"

"I'm afraid my chief wishes you off the property as soon as possible."

"Did your chief give you a reason?"

"It wasn't my place to ask for one."

The officer sat in silence as Omar finished his food. They stood up when he was finished, leaving the tray and wrappers for the cleaning person to pick up. Omar picked up his water as they walked to the eastern exit.

Looking around, Chief Hernandez saw that the Promenade was preparing for a festival as well. It wasn't as far along setting up as Alameda, but white and blue bunting was going up. Small flags were being handed out showing white fields with blue roses. He hadn't noticed before, but sure enough, mixed in the crowd here and there were persons dressed in white, the heads veiled. They were harder to spot in the more densely populated Promenade, but they were there. Two by two walking about, Promenade Security close behind, not sure what to make of them. A look of worry on their faces. Drinks were being passed around. The general feel in the facility was getting rowdy and jubilant. Omar grabbed a passing bottle and took a swing. He offered it to the security officer, who refused before taking another swing and handing back to the Promenade resident, who had handed it to him.

"Freedom." The Promenade resident saluted Omar as they took the bottle back.

"Enough of that now," the security officer barked at the resident.

Chief Hernandez attempted small talk. "So, what's this festival about?"

"Not sure. The Tribunal went silent. Can't track any of them down. Local residents say it is to celebrate Lucia's Day. I've never heard of it. You?"

"Who's paying for all this?"

"Not corporate, I can tell you that. I think that's what's got the chief nervous. Is it like this at your place?"

"No. All's quiet on my end." Chief Hernandez hoped the lie was believed. Omar wanted to get the hell out of the Promenade as fast as possible and didn't want to give the officer any reason to keep him here longer than necessary.

They pushed their way in silence the rest of the way. Chief Hernandez's eyes flicked from scene to scene as they walked. Things were heating up for the festival. Festival goers were openly drinking, vaping, or using other controlled substances. Music blared out of dark doorways leading to party rooms. Through the madness Omar got a sense that someone was following them.

The security officer was tense. Chief Hernandez could tell that officer's eyes were trying to track the goings-on as well.

A couple of feet from the exit door, they stopped.

"Hold up a second." The security guard grabbed Omar by his coat sleeve. He placed his other hand on his sidearm.

"Sorry, Mr. Hernandez, but it looks like a change of plans. I'm going to need you to hand over your—" Before the officer could finish his request, two drunk men ran into him and started fighting. The force with which they crashed into the security officer was enough for the guard to drop his grip and spill to the floor. Omar took the opportunity to slip through the door.

11:15 a.m.

Omar wasn't fine enough to run yet, and the food wasn't exactly sitting well in his stomach. He walked with intent as he weaved in and out of the bungalows, trying to make it to the street corner as fast as possible. With any luck, they would drop his pursuit there. As he made it to the corner, he took the first green crosswalk. Omar heard yelling behind him but didn't stop to look back. Omar didn't wait for the light to change, hitting the next corner. He attempted a light jog across the street between moving cars. His legs ached and felt like they may give out, but he made it to the far corner of the street, out of Promenade Security's jurisdiction.

The corner opposite the Promenade was an old gas station that had been transformed into a charging station. Omar crashed onto the faux grass that lined the station's perimeter. Somewhere in the chase, he had dropped his water. His respirator hung loosely around his neck as he ran. Not filtering the air had caused his lungs to burn and his breath to grow short. The respirator wasn't going to be enough. While pressing his mask to his face, Omar stumbled to the small convince store that accompanied these locations.

Through the door, he gasped for breath. Immediately, the recycled air cooled his face and eased his lungs' burden.

The automated bot rolled over. "I'm sorry, sir. But this facility and its features are for paying customers only. That includes recycled air. You are going to need to leave."

"I have credits. Just give me a second."

"According to our scans, that is not the case. However, if you feel this scan was in error, you may file a complaint at ChargingStation421@CENCOM. Complaints will be replied to no later than seventy-two hours from initial request. I can wait while you rectify the situation."

Omar brought up his account to try to figure out what was going on. Immediately upon logging in, he was notified that his funds were frozen. At the same time, they were being audited due to miscalculation of past taxes. Depending on the audit outcome, he may get access returned to him in seventy-two hours or less.

"A repeated scan has shown you have been notified of your current situation. Please, feel free to exit this business establishment or I will be forced to call a local Tactical Peace Brigade unit to respond."

Omar quickly took a hit of his wolfberry before putting the respirator back on and hurried out of the store. Some of the last words his commander had said to him looped in his mind. "You think there will be no consequences for your actions." He continued toward State, looking back over his shoulder, not sure if he could walk all the way back to Alameda. No, State was closer now and a better bet.

The mile walk to State was arduous. Omar escaped to the shadows of old trees that lined the street every chance he could. He abandoned even trying to hit the vape. Each time he took a hit he had to remove his respirator. He would suck in the harsh heated air afterwards as he readjusted the respirator. The air burned his lungs. When he finally reached State, the ominous ivy-covered steel fencing surrounding the campus only added to his scorn for the sun. Over the fence was a campus lush and fully covered with the old trees. The foliage seemed to cover every inch of the campus. He could see an immaculate world through the leaves, alien from the one he traveled through. He walked up to the gate to enter the campus.

"Where do you think you're going?" The metallic-sounding question cracked through someone's respirator.

Omar looked around to find a young twenty-year-old walking outside of campus along the fence line just behind him. The young man had light almond-brown hair tightly combed and styled with a part on the right-hand side. A crisp, white collared shirt was under the young man's sun jacket adorned with a neatly tied double Windsor navy blue and crimson tie. His tan dockers were ironed and creased in an almost military press. He wore no satchel or book bag of any kind and strolled up to Omar without a care in the world.

"I was hoping to get a word with Professor Larson."

"Do you have an appointment? Why are you walking in this heat? You look like shit. Don't you have a car?"

"No, I don't have an appointment. My car broke down. It's very important to speak with her. And do you always pepper strangers with a list of questions?"

"Yes, I find people fascinating. So, a critical meeting that you don't have an appointment for. Interesting. Did this professor do something wrong?"

"Look, I really need to be going. Are you some kind of security?"

"Security? No. You're not getting on campus through there, though. State Police, who you can recognize from the full tactical ballistic gear and guns, will pick you up and kick you back out. Regardless of your CENCOM Security rank, Chief. Fresno State is private property."

Shocked by the chief reference, Omar looked at the young man bewildered.

"Your rank is on your collar. Look, I'm not supposed to be out here either and you are not supposed to be on campus. I'll make you a deal. You tell me what this professor did, and I'll get you on campus. Oh, and try not to lie. You're not very good at it."

"After you." Omar saddled up next to the young man. "May I ask you some questions first?"

The young man shot out his hand to receive a handshake. "My name is David." Omar shook his hand.

"Chief Omar Hernandez. You can call me Omar. You are very astute."

"And your next question was going to be why am I not allowed off campus."

"Yes. Are you dangerous or something?" Omar chuckled to himself.

"Maybe I am." David laughed with Omar. "It's not as dramatic as all that really. The university is its own corporate entity separate from the surrounding CENCOM properties. Everything the student body does belongs to State. That causes problems for CENCOM's streaming services. Every student that attends is allowed a closely monitored allotment of travel between the two corporate entities. When abused, it causes a considerable amount of legal strain, intellectual copyright laws being what they are. At least that was how it was explained to me when I got my privileges revoked." David looked back down the road Omar had just traveled down.

"Down the street is one of CENCOM's housing communities. I'm a researcher who was not given permission to research their facility. Needless to say, I am no longer allowed to leave campus without prior authorization, which, as I mentioned, I no longer have. Now it is your turn." David walked and talked through his space as a man who knew who he was and what he was doing. A cockiness that only exists in youth.

"Yesterday, one of my residents was murdered."

"Yes, Lucia. Do you think her professor had something to do with it?"

Chief Hernandez stopped and held out both hands palm out. "What the fuck?"

"Omar, try to keep up. I do research on CENCOM's facilities and its inhabitants. Lucia is the only student on campus who lived in one of those facilities. Of course, I knew her. She was almost as smart as me. Her death is the world's loss, not just Alameda's. Do you think that the professor is somehow involved?"

"For right now, I just have a tip that I should talk with them. I've got nothing to suggest the professor did anything."

"Well, I'll tell you this, Omar. It wouldn't make sense for her professor to kill her."

"Why's that?"

"Lucia's research belonged to State. Even if she tried to steal her own work back, the school would be able to confiscate it very easily and sue her into oblivion. As I said, Lucia is almost as smart as me. She would never have been so foolish to even attempt that. Her contracts were very complicated but ironclad. Here we are."

With his left hand, David reached into his coat pocket and pulled out a small pen-size device and plunged it into some of the ivy foliage. Omar heard a click and then a motor as the ivy pulled away. An opening about the size that would allow a car to pass through opened before his very eyes.

"This entrance was used to bring equipment back and forth across the street when this school still did sporting events. It's monitored by Fresno State's streaming services. Not very closely since it's never used. Regardless I augmented the feed for my own purposes."

"You hacked it."

"Hacking is a dirty word, Omar. It implies criminal intent. I take issue with not walking where and when I like when I haven't committed a crime. As they say, only the educated are free. Shall we?"

Omar and David walked through the gate. David turned around with the little pen and closed the gate behind them before removing his respirator. Chief Hernandez was inundated with end-user agreements the university required him to sign as a guest on their campus. Omar quickly agreed to the terms, not wanting to cause any alarm and draw State Police's attention.

"You can take your respirator off. The whole campus is climate controlled."

Omar took his respirator off and looked in wonderment around the campus. It looked like a perfect day. Birds were chirping and fluttering about. The air was a perfect mix of temperature and humidity. The flowers growing in the yard added a sweet fragrance to it. Not a morsel of trash anywhere. Everything was perfectly manicured right down to the student body Omar saw off in the distance, who all seemed to be wearing suits and ties or long dresses. Omar looked down at his own attire.

"As long as you're with me, you'll be fine. I'll escort you to the professor's building. It's the least I can do for Lucia."

Everything took Omar's breath away, and he grabbed a tree to steady himself. Fumbling for his vape, he dropped it.

Omar sat down at the tree base and worked to catch his breath.

"I need to rest for a bit. Is that okay with you?"

"Sure. Let me get you something to drink."

A short trot over to a vending machine, and David was back with a couple of bags of water. David handed Omar the larger of the two bags and sat down next to him. Omar drank the bag greedily, staring up into the tree between sips, still trying to catch his breath.

David picked up Omar's vape and inspected it. Examining it, he ejected the cartridge and looked at it before putting back in.

"Interesting. When do you need your next hit?"

"Right now, as soon as I catch my breath."

"Don't use it while on campus. State Police will pick it up and arrest you. Best to wait. Can you?"

"Yeah, I think so."

"Good."

"Why is it like this?" Omar asked.

"Why is what like what now?"

"This school, State. Why is everything out there"—Omar gestured back to the gate they had just walked through— "a hellscape and this school"—Omar looked at his HUD—"thirty degrees cooler?"

"It's because of the AG dome. One of the perks, I guess, of going to school is that it is hyper-focused on agriculture and the environment. There are filters and blowers and environmentally friendly non-refrigerant-based coolers. So, they say. All of which is experimental and none of which is cheap."

They sat while Omar worked his way through the first bag of water. David played with Omar's vape, fascinated by its design. After a long silence, David, unable to contain himself in the silence finally spoke.

"Exciting news about that Grand Duchess of Desh, huh? You guys in Alameda must be busy, busy, busy!"

"What do you mean?" Omar.

"Lady Desh's return. It's all over the news. Alameda is going to have one hell of a party."

"The party is for Lucia. I don't know how Lady Desh showing her face has anything to do with Lucia's funeral," Omar said with a bit of disgust.

"Well, it's all over! People are streaming in from all over the world, eager to see if she will make another appearance at the party. Alameda's viewership has skyrocketed. Most of those feeds, of course, belong to CENCOM, but the residents did put up a non-profit feed for donations that I hear is doing very well."

The water suddenly tasted bitter in Chief Hernandez's mouth.

"We should be going." He grabbed his vape from David and stood up.

Omar and David made their way across campus. According to Omar's HUD, he still had about a mile to hike. To change the subject, Omar pointed to a group of students sitting in the grass going over a holographic chart.

"So, what are they studying over there?"

David looked. "It's not a class. They're forming a club. Professors can be terminated for moving their classes out of their assigned space without specific scientific purposes. Looks like they're forming an art club around twentieth-century urban graffiti artists."

"Why aren't teachers allowed to teach outside?"

"I don't know. There just aren't."

"So, David, what do you study here? What's your great contribution to agriculture?"

"I'm not a farmer. I'm a miner. I find new and interesting ways to utilize the data organizations like CENCOM collect. I hold three patents. Well, I mean, I came up with various systems that resulted in patents. The university actually owns them. The price of a good education, you know?" There was an air of frustration in David's tone that Omar picked up.

"Ugh."

The two of them strolled across campus as if they didn't have a care in the world. Chief Hernandez realized it was hard to rush with the air feeling so refreshing. After the march down the street, he was feeling pretty good.

A vaguely familiar melody was being played over speakers at a volume you could just make it out through the sound of a breeze through the trees. Looking around, no one seemed to be in a hurry. Neither students nor teachers seemed panicked or stressed. Several State Police officers walked the campus, although seeming out of place in military attire compared to the relaxed feeling on the grounds. Omar got no sense of agitation when passing the cops. The sublime reality that Omar was submerged in was both intoxicating and frightening. Looking up, Omar realized David had a worried look in his eyes and his eyes tended to dart back and forth. The worry lingered just past the blazing certainty of self-righteousness that only existed in the young. Still, David seemed on guard.

"This place is all a bit unreal."

"You get used to it in time if you let yourself. I've met faculty that haven't left campus in years. Some say one professor hasn't left in decades if you can believe that."

"We have a few like that in Alameda. I can't remember the last time I left. It has to have been three to four years."

"And nobody sees a problem with this. The wheels keep on turning."

"What was that now?" Chief Hernandez asked.

"You know what, Omar? Over two hundred years ago, most people didn't leave their homes. Hardly ever straying more than a dozen miles in their entire live. Then someone invented the steam engine, and with it, the world got smaller. People left their homes in droves for the first time to see the world. We continued inventing new, faster ways to travel, and the world kept getting smaller. The world is now small enough to fit within the space of one's mind. And just like that, once again no one leaves their home."

"Looking around, I would have thought Lucia would have chosen to live on campus. I wonder why she stayed in Alameda?"

"Lucia would have said it was to stay grounded. She loved Alameda very much."

"What was she like?"

"Lucia? Well"—David smiled to himself—"she was fiercely competitive. Didn't like to back down from a challenge. Absolutely brilliant and focused. She had a bottomless capacity to place herself in other people's shoes. She wanted to feed the world."

They continued to walk in silence for the remainder of their walk.

"I have to go to my next lab appointment, Omar. It was nice meeting you. The building straight ahead is the one you want. Professor Larson is on the second floor."

Once again, David stuck out his hand to shake. Omar reached out and received the farewell gesture.

"Thank you for your help, David."

"It was my pleasure. Remember, don't use your vape until you're off campus."

"Will do."

"Oh, and Omar?"

"Yeah?" Omar turned back towards David, who flicked an augmented object to him. Reflexively Omar reached out and caught it mid-air. He looked at the small disk that someone had coded to have an animated wheat field blowing in the breeze on one side and a bulldog panting and licking its chops on the other.

"What's this?"

"Rideshare token. So, you don't have to walk back to Alameda. The vehicle will be considered part of the campus, so remember the vape. Okay?"

"Thanks."

"Freedom," David said nonchalantly as he turned away.

Omar haphazardly waved goodbye, perplexed by the farewell he received. Chalking it up to David's time at the Promenade, he slotted the token into his HUD inventory and walked into the building.

12:10 p.m.

The inside of the science building was as clean as the outside, except for the lack of greenery. The halls had a couple of students. Once again, no one rushed. A soft chatter hung in the air. It had been some years since Omar had visited a library, but that was what the hallway reminded him of. The same soft melody played throughout the building that Omar had heard while walking to the science building. He breathed in and smelled the same scent in the air. All of which brought calm to him. Omar didn't feel the urge to hit his vape. He desired answers to his questions, which motivated him but not too intensely. David's voice echoed in his mind. "You get used to it if you let it." Chief Hernandez shook his head. Fear began to climb up his spine as a realization came to mind. He was being doped. That's why everyone was calm and collected. The school was pumping some kind of vape in the air. Chief Hernandez looked closer at the students. All of them looked lucid but calm. Too calm.

A small ball of panic grew in his stomach. Years of drug use had taught Omar to grab hold of that panic. Not letting it grow so big he would have a freakout but not letting the air and music chase it away. Trying to ride out the effects like a bad hit of wolfberry. Willing himself sober.

An augmented directory QR code hung in the air. Chief Hernandez scanned it and looked up directions to the room number of Professor Larson. He climbed the stairs slowly. He would elevate his heart if he rushed, thus breathing in more of the mickey vape. Linger too long, and it would be similar results. He didn't like being drugged against his will.

His heels clicked as he moved with purpose down the second-floor hall. Turning into the last room on the right, Omar reached the professor's office. A brunette with hazel eyes sat behind an old worn wood desk in front of a door. She was wearing a rainbow-colored blouse with a starched white collar. She looked up, confused.

"Umm… are you lost or something?"

"Yes, I'm looking for Professor Larson."

"Doctor Larson doesn't have any appointments scheduled today. Is she expecting you?"

"No. I'm dropping in, but it's essential. My name is Chief Hernandez. I'm a security officer with the Alameda community."

"Oh, Lucia's home. I'll let the doctor know, but she is pretty busy today. You may have to wait."

Omar looked around and saw an old wooden chair sitting against the wall's far side. He sat down. "I'll wait. I must speak with her."

The small antechamber had no decorations. The walls were completely blank. It was home to the desk and three old wood chairs. The furniture was a natural wood grain with a varnish that was well worn where hands would rest. As plain as they looked, Omar knew real wooden furniture was expensive, and these pieces, although he wasn't an expert in the field, would more than likely have come from when the college was first built, making the chair his butt currently sat in worth hundreds of thousands of dollars. He shimmied in his seat. A hundred thousand dollars or not, it was not very comfortable.

The longer he sat, the harder it was for Omar to hold on to his ball of panic. He kept pulling his vape out and looking at it. He wasn't sure if he could go to the restroom and take a hit, but the thought crossed his mind. Again and again. He kept tapping his heel on the floor as his leg shook, to the student's disgust. His fidgeting was getting on her nerves. Finally, after an hour, a male student came in and took her place behind the desk. He was wearing a blue jumper with a yellow t-shirt underneath that was, to Omar's delight, a bit small accentuating the young man's arms. The two students chatted for a moment, too quietly for Omar to make out the conversation, then she left down the hall. The new student laid his hands palms down on the desk. The student stared off into oblivion as he busied himself with whatever task he needed to accomplish. The lowered lids of fluttering eyes deep in virtual reality communicated a clear don't-talk-to-me vibe. This left Omar trying to entertain himself again. Omar was scared to go online and burn up some time in a digital trance as he would not concentrate on holding off the effects of the mickey vape. He looked around the room.

He hadn't noticed it before, but a side door led to the room next door. An augmented text floated over the door that read "Lab" in bold red font. Above the door was a clock with a large face on it. It was an old clock with a yellowing face and fading numbers. A stainless-steel ring ran the circumference of the clock. It was swept gracefully across the face thirteen seconds behind Omar's HUD clock. The room walls were brick, covered in thick white paint that gave them a puffy look to their edges. Here and there, the paint had chipped off only to be painted over again. It gave the surface of each brick a unique topographical landscape from its fellow bricks. Holes were sparse and dispersed on the wall. Chief Hernandez assumed it was for hanging old equipment that was no longer needed.

Omar began to occupy himself by making out shapes and faces he thought he could see in the wall's white textured paint. He thought about the short interaction he had with David. David must have known about the mickey vape. That would explain why he had that look in his eye. Going off campus would have given him enough distance to know that the university was experimenting on the student body. *Or was it simple manipulation?* he thought. It would also explain why Lucia chose to live off campus. But why not tell someone? Maybe she had? Or was going to and that is why she was killed.

Just when he about had enough, as Omar got up to leave, the door to the lab opened and a woman who looked about as tired as Omar felt walked out.

"Professor Larson?" Omar asked.

"Yes?" The woman turned to face Omar.

"I'm Chief Hernandez from Alameda. I wanted to speak with you."

"Oh, right. Right this way please. Sorry for keeping you waiting but we have a pretty big emergency on our hands." She opened the door to her office. "Please, come in and have a seat."

Omar followed her in, "I'm sorry if I have come at a bad time. You're in the midst of an emergency?" Chief Hernandez asked.

"Yes. Well, we just received a huge grant for our research, and I just lost my primary researcher. Lucia was an exceptional individual and I'm scrambling to fill a tremendous void. Terrible loss. Just a terrible loss. Such a brilliant young woman. Her breakthrough in our research has solidified this department's grant from CENCOM for the next ten years."

"Well, that's kind of why I came down here. I was hoping you could maybe be able to shine a light on what she was doing. I've seen the gardens." Omar paused as he remembered Grandfather hanging from the trellis. "And it all looks amazing."

"Amazing?! Oh, yes. Before Lucia's breakthrough, some were beginning to believe whether it was even possible to achieve the goal. The lab was under threat of being closed down. My life's work would have been a footnote in scientific research. The goal was to achieve yield losses as low as .01%, no pesticides, a reduction in water consumption, and most importantly, increased pollination with a decrease in bee population. For years we made little progress on one or two of the items but all four?" the professor said. "Sorry, it's hard not to get excited over it."

"That's all right. Professor Larson, you should know that's part of the reason I'm here is that I can't figure out why anyone would want to kill Lucia."

"I see. I want to show you something then. I already sent a copy to a detective from Tac. Lucia would send me these updates about her lab at Alameda. She would have to come down to the school to work, but she was allowed to collect data at Alameda. The resulting crops belonging to the residents incentivized the populous to contribute to our research, increasing our data collection tenfold. My lab was running out of resources but with Alameda's help we had more crops to test."

The professor looked off into space. Omar could tell she was going through a filing system.

"Here is the stream she sent me from one of our labs on campus."

Omar received a temporary shared file that he opened and viewed. In front of him was Lucia. She was half-sitting, half-squatting on a stool leaning into the feed. She was surrounded by a beige lab with various machinery around her. Behind her was a clear windowed wall. Omar could see students walking back and forth through the window. Lucia was smiling. Her hair was pulled back into a bun with what looked like half a chopstick keeping it in place. She was wearing brown coveralls with a plaid long-sleeved t-shirt underneath. Her eyes sparkled with life.

"Hey, Rhonda. Here's this week's data. But first, I've got a new one for you. How do nerves communicate? I'll let you think for a minute." Lucia began singing the *Jeopardy* theme song with do-dos. "Ready? How do nerves communicate? With cellular phones!"

The young woman started to laugh and snort at her own joke. Omar didn't get the joke but couldn't help but chuckle along with her. Lucia was just… she was goofy. An unexpected quality after what everyone was saying about her. The professor across the table began to cry.

"I'm sorry, Chief. That was the wrong day. As you can see, she was so wonderful. Sorry, give me a moment." The professor looked off for a moment, "Here is the stream I received three days ago."

A new file came up, and Omar started to watch it. The image was very different than the one Omar had just finished watching. Lucia was hunched over with her hair down, almost covering her face. She was now wearing a blue coveralls. The bright and happy face was replaced with dark and stressed eyes that darted back and forth. It reminded Omar of how David looked earlier.

"Good evening, Professor Larson. I need you to look at this data and get back to me. I found a variant code in the air samples. I believe that I figured it out, but I would like a third opinion on the code. I gave it to another to see if he would get similar results. If my findings are correct. Someone has been intentionally sterilizing the population of Alameda. I've—"

Omar paused the feed. In the background was a blurred image he had stopped. Rewound the feed ten seconds and played again to be sure. The figure crossed the window behind Lucia, briefly paused, and rolled their shoulders in a too familiar way. Omar played it back one more time. He was certain it was Jack. Omar's blood ran cold.

Omar swallowed hard. "What does she mean sterilizing?" he asked.

"It means that the code she mentioned is decreasing the population of Alameda by preventing reproduction."

"And you got similar results?"

"Yeah, it's why I sent it to the detective when he came by asking questions. He said not to worry about it. It didn't seem to have anything to do with her death but that he would run it up the chain nonetheless."

Omar wiped the sweat from his brow. He was scared to actually hear what he knew the professor would say.

"Professor Larson, what was the detective's name?"

"Um… a Detective Williams."

"Thank you for your time. I need to go."

Omar scrambled from his seat and headed for the door.

"Well, if there's anything else?" he heard from the professor as he raced out of the office. Whatever mickey was in the air was no match for pure rage. He brought up his HUD and found the nearest student rideshare park. One was located just outside the building on Barstow that runs parallel to the campus.

* * *

Omar hopped into the first empty vehicle he could find. Handing over the token to the UI, he yelled, "Alameda, south entrance."

Omar tried to bring up the occupants list in Alameda to see if Jack was still there. The directory wouldn't load for him. No error message provided. It just didn't load. He tried to call Security Officer Wright. It was sent to voicemail. He hung up without leaving a message. Omar texted him.

[Chief.Sec.O.HERNANDEZ]: @Sec.Off.J.WRIGHT I believe Detective Williams killed Lucia and possibly Grandfather. Please, meet me at the south entrance. I'll be there in 5.

Omar sat back in the car. Nervous energy flowed through him as he tried to figure out how to approach this new discovery. He grabbed his vape, anxious to take a hit. David had warned him, though, and he couldn't take any chances to be stopped right now. Not for something as fucking stupid as a vape. Alameda couldn't come soon enough.

The student rideshare vehicle pulled up to the south entrance, and Omar jumped out and ran to the door. As soon as he was out of the car, he took a hit from his vape. Fritz was waiting for him inside by the door.

"Fuck, you're predictable. You can't be here, Omar. Put your hat on and keep your head down. You need to come with me. I know where I can hide you." Fritz stopped him, cramming the dongle into Omar's hand in a way that it couldn't have been picked up by cameras.

"Hide me. What? I know who killed Lucia. He's still in Alameda. I'm going to go grab that sonovabitch right now."

Fritz pulled Omar to the side before reaching the stairs and ducked down behind the railing. Omar noticed Fritz kept looking over their shoulder.

"No, Omar. You have to get the fuck out of here. CENCOM's been playing a stream of you killing Lucia. I'm going to try and get you out of here."

Omar looked down at the USB dongle.

"Fritz, did you figure out what is on this thing?"

"Not yet. But if Lucia's notes are correct, I'm not sure I want to. It is definitely a vape code. Military-grade. Very clean script. Now come on, we're going to El Corazon. I'll see if I can't get you some help but you ne—"

"Freeze!"

"Fuck!" Fritz yelled.

Five Alameda Security Officers led by Johnny surrounded Omar and Fritz. Their guns were already drawn and trained on the two of them. Johnny walked up, pulled Omar's gun, and handed it to one of the officers while Omar tried to palm the dongle. Johnny grabbed his wrist and took the dongle.

"I'll take that, thank you," Johnny said. "You really make me sick. These poor people trusted you, Omar."

"Johnny, I didn't kill anyone."

Johnny struck Omar across the face. "Not another fucking word."

A crowd started to form.

"Omar Hernandez, you are being detained for the murder of Lucia Vitores."

"What the fuck are you guys doing? I didn't kill Lucia. Detective Williams did. You have to let me go."

"Bo. Murry. Take Fritz to holding. See what he knows. We'll head to the detention center through the corridors. We don't want the residents to get riled up."

An officer came up and grabbed Omar from behind. Omar struggled but received a gut punch from Johnny for his efforts. Another stripped him of his respirator and coat. They dragged him to the nearest maintenance door. An empty bottle flew past Omar's head and he tried to duck. Omar turned to see a crowd forming around him and the security officers. Hate filled the crowd's eyes as they started to yell at him.

"It's the chief!" a resident called out.

"Fuck you, Chief!"

More trash flew through the air. With his arms being held, Omar's attempts to avoid the pelting were in vain.

"Lucia was one of us, you piece of shit!" another resident yelled.

"How could you?"

A brick hit Omar in the head, causing a gash to form and blood to pour down his face.

"All right, get back. We have him. It's over."

Another brick flew through the air.

"Goddammit! Just get him inside. We'll cuff him in there," Security Officer Wright called out, pushing back to protect himself and the team.

"Chief! Chief!" Omar heard over the crowd. He spotted Fritz in the back of the mob.

"I didn't do it, Fritz. Find me some help! I didn't do it!" Omar yelled out.

Once in the corridor, the barrage of raining debris ceased. The maintenance corridor was tight. The small ensemble made their way north. As they were just coming up to a T-intersection, Chief Hernandez made a move for it. He slammed the officer on his right into the wall, freeing his hands. Omar swung and cracked the officer on his left in the jaw. Omar grabbed his pistol and chambered a round. Pointing it at Johnny.

"Don't even think about it," Omar shouted.

Security Officer Johnny Wright's hand landed on his sidearm just as Omar's round caught Johnny in the right shoulder. Johnny spun in recoil as he hit the ground.

"I didn't kill her," Omar shouted as he took off down the corridor. He headed for the first door he could find. Ran into it only for it not to open. He pulled out his RFID keys. Still, the door wouldn't open. Omar kept running, checking door after door. A shot rang out, and Omar felt like he caught a bullet in his left arm. He studied it on the move to find it was only grazed. He turned left and found two Alameda guards dressed in their strange white garb, guns drawn, heading his way.

"Hold up, Chief," they called out.

Not giving the vigilantes a chance to draw a bead on him, Omar fired a wild shot as he turned and ran away as fast as he could, inspecting every door he passed.

As he ran farther away, he heard shooting. But it sounded farther the faster he ran down the corridor. Frantically checking doors, Omar found each one locked. Omar staggered around one final corner to find the corridor dead-end at the base of a ladder. The ladder to the roof led to a landing with a door. Omar knew this door was always unlocked. He holstered his gun and tried to climb as fast as he could. He made it to the top without anyone taking a shot at him.

It was only after Omar was through the door and he heard the electric lock click behind him that he realized his mistake. He was trapped on the roof.

Omar went to pull on his respirator only to remember that it wasn't there. Immediately, he started to gasp for air. The sun pelted him. The hottest part of the day, and he was standing in the hottest place in Alameda. He looked for shade or some-place to hide from the sun, but there was none to be found. The roof was covered in large industrial coolers and solar panels. The industrial coolers were steel behemoths. The solar panels lay on the roof flat. Both the coolers and the panels reflected the sun into Omar's eyes. Everything was covered in bird shit. Omar pulled his firearm out and fell into cover next to a cooler.

"I really was rooting for you, Omar." Jack's voice came in over Omar's HUD. "From the beginning, really. When I found out you were the onsite chief, I thought this would be great. Working alongside each other again. I don't know. I thought maybe... maybe you could have returned to Tac. Returned to me."

Omar looked around. Frantically, he searched for Jack. The intense sun blinded him from making anything out. Omar moved to another cooler and another trying to find some kind of tactical advantage that allowed him to block some of the sun as he desperately scanned to find Jack.

"What the fuck, Jack? Why me?"

"You always had to do things on hard mode, didn't you? Come on out, Omar. We'll talk." Jack's voice came from near the door Omar had just gone through. Now a couple of coolers away.

Omar attempted to bring up the roof feed only to be notified that his access had been denied. He made his way to the next cooler and peeked around the edge. Ducking and weaving, he moved to another cooler unit. As Omar leaned on the cooler, the shit-covered sheet metal radiated heat that seeped past his clothes and burned his skin.

"If you had just played ball, man. This kills me, Omar. It really does. But I made the decision since you pulled that bullshit back in Madera. It was always going to be me over you. Shit, me over anyone really."

"Are you kidding me? You killed Lucia because of Madera?" Omar moved to the Solar panel, squatting down to see if he could see Detective William's feet.

Jack let out a long exhale. "God, you're conceited. It wasn't supposed to be anyone. Lucia was to be just another dead girl in a long line of dead mall rats. You found something, though. Something we overlooked. That changed everything. Now that the USB drive is in Johnny's custody, we can figure out what she thought she was planning to do with it. I'm assuming your little friend Fritz made a copy. So, he's going to have a little accident, too."

Omar jumped out from behind the solar panel and ran to the next box for cover. A shot rang out, and Omar's gun exploded in his hand. Looking to see where the shot came from, he turned in time to see Jack shoot him in his right leg, just above the knee. Omar collapsed on top of a searing hot solar panel shattering the cell. His leg screamed blue and yellow through closed eyes as he crawled for cover by the roofs edge. Omar leaned against the inferno.

"A death sentence just for finding that thing?"

"Not at first. CENCOM had hoped you'd work with us. How's the leg?" Jack walked out from behind a cooler and strolled over to Omar. Jack drew a bead back on Omar.

Omar's leg was on fire. He reached down and tore open

his pants to find black streaks climbing from the bullet wound through his veins up his leg.

"What did you shoot me with?" Omar asked.

"You like that? It's new. It's different from what Security Officer Wright injected you with last night. That injection doesn't destroy so much as it shuts down and restarts the bots."

Jack kissed the side of his gun. "Now this shit, woowee! Straight from CENCOM R&D. You see, the problem with shooting anyone nowadays is that everyone has so many fucking bots coursing through them the bullets don't tend to work very well. What I shot you with is overloading your nanobots, one at a time. That's why I had to strangle that Lucia bitch. Didn't have these babies. Messy work, strangling. This is way better. Does it burn?"

Omar looked at William's shoes and saw the mud still caked on them.

"Your shoes are dirty. Why didn't I realize why your shoes were dirty? You killed Grandfather Sandoval."

"Yeah, well, while Johnny was taking care of you. I was sent to take care of the old man. To tell you the truth, CENCOM thought you gave the dongle to him instead of Fritz. It recorded you talking after the funeral and assumed you handed it off before going to dinner. I was pissed to find out he didn't have shit. I'm really fucking tired of this filthy fucking mall." Jack kicked Omar in the ribs.

"It was Johnny who attacked me?"

"Oh, yeah. As soon as CENCOM informed him that you were our primary suspect, he was… well, heartbroken at first. I guess he liked working with you. Upon learning our truth, he became all too eager to help."

"I found bruising all over her face. Why did you beat Lucia?"

"Interrogations are never easy, Omar. You know that. Remember the Bachinsky brothers? It took you two days to get Ivan to break."

"You've become a real sicko in your old age. Fuck you."

"You had your chance. That's rich you call me sick."

"Why me? If all you needed was the USB, why the death sentence?"

"Last night at the pub. I asked for it. You didn't hand it over. And that fucking speech you gave me. CENCOM realized you were compromised. You've really drunk the Kool-Aid. Now you need to answer my questions. What is Lady Desh planning? What does she know?"

"I don't know. I haven't been able to speak with her. All I know is she seems to be behind that weird fucking cult."

Jack shot Omar in his other leg. Omar screamed.

"I don't know, Jack. Fuck. I don't know anything!"

"Do you really think it's a cult? Are you really that stupid? It's an army. Does Lady Desh know what is on the stick drive?"

"I don't know. I don't know what is on the drive. I never got a chance to look at it. Please, don't kill me. I don't know anything."

"But you found something at the school, didn't you? CENCOM showed me you talking to Fritz. How'd you know it was me?" Jack stepped on the entry wound on Omar's leg.

Omar let out a yell as hot pain ran up his leg.

"A video. You show up in the last video Lucia submitted to her teacher. I remembered you said that you had been at State a couple of days before, and then I saw you and realized you had killed her over her discovery."

"And her discovery was?" Jack asked in a mocking voice.

Omar looked at Jack. Long gone was the man he loved. All he saw now was personified evil walking around in the husk of the man he once knew. Omar straightened himself up.

"She believed someone was sterilizing the Alameda population."

Jack let out an exasperated breath. "Someone, Omar? No. CENCOM. But you knew that, didn't you? Deep down in that shriveled, disgusting body, there is still a detective trying to come out. And that's the difference between life in prison and death. I know it seems cold, but CENCOM doesn't just kill for kicks and giggles. If you had just left well enough alone…" Jack stopped and looked off in the distance. Shaking his head in agreement.

"All right. CENCOM believes you don't know anything about Lady Desh. They're sighting you running away from those freaks as proof you are not in league with them. I'm not so sure, but you've got to trust the AI. Looks like CENCOM finally wrapped up the last edit of you killing Mr. Sandoval. We're ready to begin. You know you should be thanking me. Everyone who sees these last images of you won't be so disgusted at how you look. You look good with your face augmented on my body. CENCOM is telling everyone that you killed both of them in a drug-fueled rage, by the way. Let me show you what we are now streaming to everyone in Alameda."

Omar was exhausted. He looked down at his legs. Through the tear, he saw that his right leg had turned completely black. His left leg leaked blood that dried as soon as it hit the hot surface of the roof. Every inch of Omar burned from the sun and the bot-killing code. He felt his breathing growing shallower.

A picture popped up in Omar's HUD. It looked staticky and unclear as Omar's bots slowly died, one by one, inside him. A supercut stream of what looked like Omar strangling Lucia was playing. After that, one started up of Omar carrying her body wrapped in an old tarp into Alameda. Followed by a final stream of Omar hanging Grandfather in the garden. Jack's habit of rolling his shoulders to straighten his posture was obvious to anyone who knew him.

"Aaaannnd your execution order just came in now that it's official. Sorry, Omar. Just following orders." Jack cleared his throat. "Omar Hernandez," he began formally, articulating every syllable, "video evidence has been retrieved in the murder of Lucia Vitores that proves that while in a drug-fueled state, you killed her with your bare hands. Furthermore, the following night, evidence has come forth that while mixing wolfberry and nighthowler, two controlled narcotic vapes, you went on a bender and murdered Mr. Miguel Sandoval. CENCOM's judiciary committee reviewed the footage and your action therein and has determined that you are to be terminated immediately. Do you have any last requests?"

Omar looked up at the man he once loved.

"Jack, you don't have to do this. Look at me. You know what happened to me. This is what happens to those who follow CENCOM's orders blindly."

"No, Omar. You are what happens when you grow a conscious."

BANG.

Made in United States
Orlando, FL
16 August 2022

21126248R00093